The Fated Sky

OTHER TITLES BY HENRIETTA BRANFORD

White Wolf

Fire, Bed, and Bone

Dimanche Diller

Dimanche Diller in Danger

Dimanche Diller at Sea

Chance of Safety

Spacebaby

Spacebaby and the Mega-Volt Monster

The Fated Sky

HENRIETTA BRANFORD

CANDLEWICK PRESS
CAMBRIDGE, MASSACHUSETTS

First U.S. edition 1999

Branford, Henrietta, date.
The fated sky / Henrietta Branford.—1st ed.
p.   cm.
Summary: Ran, a sixteen-year-old Viking girl, struggles to control
the events of her life and escape from the death that is supposed
to be her destiny.
ISBN 0-7636-0775-4
[1. Vikings—Fiction. 2. Iceland—Fiction.] I. Title
PZ7.B737385Fat   1999
[Fic]—dc21   98-51120

2 4 6 8 10 9 7 5 3 1

Printed in the United States of America

This book was typeset in Weiss.

Candlewick Press
2067 Massachusetts Avenue
Cambridge, Massachusetts 02140

Our remedies oft in ourselves do lie,

Which we ascribe to heaven. The fated sky

Gives us free scope, only doth backward pull

Our slow designs when we ourselves are dull.

—*All's Well that Ends Well*, Act I, scene 1

ONE

THERE WAS A DRAGON in the sky the night
before the stranger came. It flamed across the red west
from the cliffs to the black road of the sea. Its jaws were
open, showing its curved teeth tinged with yellow. The sin-
gle eye it turned toward me glowed like an ember in the
darkness of its face. I watched it while the sun went down,
and its body bleached from fire to gold to crumpled leather.
I watched it till the sun was gone. It must have slid down to
the land of ice then, because I could see no more of it. But
all the time I saw it in the sky, I know it saw me too. Its red
eye watched my gray eye. It did not speak to me. But I
feared it.

In the morning when I woke, I felt a new thing around
my neck. Someone had hung a little silver hammer there to
bring me luck and keep me safe.

Amma, my grandmother, got up while it was dark, but I
could always find her. I would run down to the beach and

see the dark shape of her, with her thick cloak moving in the breeze, her back to the big rock and her face to the ocean. She liked to stand there and think about my grandfather. That rock is where she stood to watch him leave, the last time that he sailed away.

Perhaps he feasts with Ran now. Perhaps my father and my brothers feast there with him. Or if they all died fighting, they'll be in Odin's great hall. I hope they didn't die some other way and go down to the land of Hel. I doubt if there's much feasting at her table.

"Amma!" I shouted. "Amma! Look what Thor has brought me in the night!"

I knew, and Amma knew I knew, that it was she who put the hammer there. But with Amma I spoke as I felt. And I felt sure that Thor had made her do it because he cared for me. I was a child then, though I was sixteen.

My name is Ran. Amma named me Ran because I love the sea—and maybe for my stormy temper. Ran is the goddess of the sea; she pulls the drowning sailors down to her great hall at the bottom of the ocean. Sometimes I hate my name because it's hers, but Amma says I mustn't.

"The gods do what they must do, Ran," she used to say, "the same as us."

"Why be a god then, Amma?" I would ask.

"They are who they must be. Now stand here and pay attention. The border of your weaving's a disgrace."

We were not rich, my people, but we were not poor. We had our fields and the fishing from the sea. We kept cattle, half a dozen, sheep and three pigs, goats, and a flock of chickens. And Bor, my father's horse, though he was already old then. Our farm was called Smolsund. We had no slaves and only one servant to help us, an old man we called Od.

TWO

AMMA KISSED ME and admired my pendant. Then she told me to go back indoors because a storm was coming in from the ocean. I looked and presently, above the waves, where the dragon had burned the night before, black clouds came flying in toward the land.

When I turned to run back up the little slope to our house, there was a stranger there. He had jumped down from his horse and was standing with his back to the dawn and his face to our door. My mother stood in the doorway with the early morning light shining on her face, and he was staring at her. He put out a hand to touch her, then drew it back. She leaned forward a little, kissed him, and leaned back, as if to study what effect this might have on him. Because of the way he stood and looked at her, not moving, not speaking, full of longing, I saw her for the first time as a stranger might. She was beautiful, but angry.

The stranger's name was Vigut. His name was ugly but his looks were very fine. He had bright, fierce eyes and glossy dark hair. His beard was thick and wavy, and his teeth, though broken, looked strong and white. Everything about him looked strong—his stiff blue cloak, his high leather boots, his belt with the bronze strap-end stamped with a wolf's face, and especially his sword.

The horse did not look quite so smooth and sleek as the master. His head hung down as if he was too tired to raise it, and his coat was dark and coiling into sweaty curls. Foam dropped from his mouth and his rump was marked where Vigut had beaten him.

"Ran," my mother called. "Take our guest's horse to Od. Tell him to bring more peat for our fire when the horse is stabled."

"And tell your Od to rub my horse down properly," Vigut added. "He's not to be fed or watered till he's rested."

Od would know that, I wanted to say. Od isn't stupid. But I took the horse's reins and led him into the barn without speaking. I could smell his hot salt sweat, and I felt with my hand on his neck how his muscles trembled.

Od took him from me. He heaved off the leather saddle and slipped the bit out of the horse's mouth. He twisted a handful of straw in one hand and began to rub the animal down, starting with his chest and working slowly around under his belly, up across his back, and down each leg.

"He says you mustn't feed the horse, or water him yet," I said. Od raised one eyebrow. "I'm only saying what he said." Od raised the other eyebrow. "And when you've seen to him, mother wants peat for the fire. And there'll be food soon."

I ran back indoors, knowing there would be work for me

to do. Our house had stone walls, and a roof of green, growing turf. I thought our roof posts very good, all carved with stories—but then I'd seen no others. The big pot was already hanging over the fire, with beans and carrots and onions stewing. Amma was gutting the fish I'd caught with my hook and line the night before, with Fugle, her tomcat, winding himself around her legs expectantly. My mother was grinding barley for bread. Both of them were weeping. My mother nodded to me to take over from her and went to pour beer for our guest.

I knew from the way she passed him the horn that my life was changing. I could feel the doors of my childhood closing behind me, and the cold wind of hardship blowing in my face. I caught Amma's old eye and she winked. Slow, child, is what the wink meant. Be careful. I am not good at being careful.

When Vigut praised our drinking horn—where you put your lips to drink was overlaid with silver—I answered him, though he had spoken to my mother, not to me. "My father brought it back from the east," I said.

My mother shook her head.

"He is trading there now," I continued recklessly, "and this time, when he returns, he will bring mother a necklace of crystal and carnelian, and me a hunting dog."

Vigut said nothing, and my mother turned toward me with a strange look, somewhere between cruelty and pity. "Your father feasts with Ran under the sea," she said. "Your brothers too. I have known it for a long time. Vigut, our visitor, knows it too. He heard it from a sailor who saw their ship go down."

I stood up slowly and looked from my mother's face to Amma. I could not see Amma's face. She was bent forward, with her forehead on her knees. I threw down my cup and made a sign to avert evil.

"He's a liar!" I shouted. "He's a liar and a thief!" It was only then, while I was shouting, that I realized I'd still hoped, always hoped, that my father would return and bring my brothers safe home too.

My mother took a stick from the pile of firewood and struck my hand hard so that I pulled it back and clamped it, stinging, underneath my arm. "Get out," she hissed. "If I'm to have no sons, I'll have no daughter either. Give your company to the beasts tonight. They will enjoy it more than I do."

I ran, not looking at Amma, not looking at my mother. I felt ashamed, ashamed of having been so rude. And stupid, too. If I had longed secretly for my father to return, how much more must my mother have longed to see her sons sail home again?

I did not know my father well. He was often away from Smolsund, and when he was with us at home he spent his time with my brothers, not with me. But he stood between my mother's anger and myself when he was there, and I loved him for that. Her two sons had been my mother's only joy.

THREE

IT WAS A LONG and bitter night. It would have been much worse if Amma had not crept out to comfort me. She covered me with her fur cloak and lay down beside me. I lay with my head throbbing, the skin of my face stretched tight and my eyes swollen and sore.

My father used to travel far inland and bring back furs and slaves and silver. We never saw these things at Smolsund. He took them to the great port of Birka and sold them. We never saw the money that they fetched either. He'd spent that, or most of it, long before he came back home to us. He and my mother fought about it often. Amma would sigh and press her lips together and hunt for Fugle's fleas to crack them with her fingernails. I knew that she blamed my mother. I did, too. If she would only be friends with my father, I used to think, he'd bring the money home.

Well, that was all past now. His ship had sunk and he was gone, him and my brothers too.

Amma and I did not sleep much that night. Toward dawn she got slowly up, rubbing her aching bones, and went indoors. It would not have done for my mother to find her comforting me.

I lay in the hay close to my father's old horse, bitten and stung by things I couldn't see, watching the light come up. The pigs scuffled and pushed and grunted; every now and then the boar would nip one of the sows and she would squeal. I thought of my mother, warm in the hall with Vigut. I fingered my silver hammer and asked Thor to help me.

"Please Thor," I said, "speak to the goddess Freya, who looks after women. Ask her to send my father home. If she will do that for me, she can ask me to do anything for her, and I will do it. Please, Thor, ask her to do this for me. And please, Thor, ask her to make my mother ugly in Vigut's sight."

In the morning, when Od came to fetch me in—my mother sent Od for me, as if I were a servant or an animal—I saw at once that Thor had not been listening to the last part of my prayer. Or if he had, the goddess had not. Vigut watched my mother all around the hall. And she was not weeping as a widow should.

My mother's name was Astrid. She had yellow hair, heavy and thick and straight. Her eyes were very dark, and you couldn't tell what she was thinking by looking at them. Some people shout when they are angry. My father did that. Some will slap you or shake you. My mother was one of those who grows still and quiet with anger.

When I came into the hall that morning, she was happy.

She ought to have been weeping for my father, but every movement of her arm and shoulder, as she pounded barley for our bread, announced her joy.

When she looked up and saw me, all her pleasure drained away. I knew why. She had told me often that when she saw me, she saw my father. I have dark hair, like his, and light eyes, and my nose, although it is still small, is beginning to curve around into an eagle's beak, like his. It is not comfortable to remind a woman of the husband she didn't love. Nor to remind the living of the dead.

"Did you sleep well, child?" she asked. She meant: Remember that you made me angry yesterday. Remember not to do so today.

I nodded. I could not trust myself to speak. I took the barley flour from her, added water, and began to knead it into bread dough. Vigut watched me, smiling. I have seen kinder smiles on a serpent's face.

Amma banged about the fire, adding too much wood, making it smoke, then making it worse by blowing on it. She could not slap my mother or our guest, so she pretended Od had burned the porridge and slapped him instead. She gave me a hen's egg that she'd boiled for me. "To keep your young bones safe from winter's cold," she said, not looking at my mother.

We could not hold a proper funeral for my father and my brothers until the waiting time was over because we had no bodies by which to prove their deaths. But when we had eaten, we went out to the barn and chose something with which to honor them. My mother whistled up my father's little terrier. He struggled when the knife went in, not understanding that we sent him to his master. We prayed to Thor and raised a small mound.

Snow had fallen and we were coming to the time of year when the great sacrifices must be made to Odin, father of the gods. My mother and I had planned to cross our headland and travel around by sledge to Sessing, a neighboring farmstead, where our cousin Ristil worked. We would stay several days and take part in the winter ceremonies there. Od would stay at home to feed those animals we were keeping through the winter, and Amma would stay with him because the journey was too hard for her.

Usually we would have finished the autumn killing and the curing of the meat by then, but the weather was fine and mild that year, and we had put it off. Our animals would feed us through till spring, Amma said. Even with Vigut's appetite, she added, though not when my mother could hear her.

Of our six cows, we chose three to keep and three to kill. We had nine sheep that year and kept seven. Sheep are hardy, and if they can get no grass they will eat seaweed. Every farm must have a boar and sows for spring breeding—we had lost both litters of young to wolves that spring, so we killed only one sow, the oldest. The hens we always kept for as long as we could feed them. Not all the meat was ours, of course. We always brought a good share to the feast at Odin's sacrifice.

Last year we managed the slaughter by ourselves. It wasn't difficult. Od did the heavy work with Mother.

Amma taught me how to joint the carcasses and how to smoke and salt the meat. I had to know every part of farming. The farm had always been my mother's business; my father was never home for long enough to make it his. Vigut knew nothing of our farm. It hurt to see how Mother let him say what should be done and how and why and when, that autumn.

I asked Amma what she thought about it. We were out behind the barn, searching for hens' eggs. She was bent over, peering behind the stinging nettles. She straightened up slowly and looked at me in a thoughtful way. She put an arm across my shoulders, partly for love, partly for leaning on, and told me we would leave the eggs and go down to the sea for shellfish.

"Shall I fetch a bowl to put them in, Amma?" I asked.

She shook her head. "No need, my sprigget,"—which was what she used to call me when we were alone—"we'll put them in my shawl if we find any."

The sand was almost white on the beach at Smolsund. The rocks were dark. Usually the sea seemed to be fighting with the land. Only a few times in the summer did that beach feel gentle. Then I'd run down early, while my brothers were still eating breakfast, and slip my clothes off behind one of the rocks, and walk in the water for the joy of its smooth, live, rock and slap. Mostly, though, the beach was harsh and loud and windy. Spray soaked me, my clothes flapped, and my hair would tangle into sticky knots. That's how it was that morning. Amma leaned across my shoulders, and I put my arm round her middle, and we made our way over to our sitting place, between two rocks, out of the wind.

"It's time I talked to you about our guest," she said. "What has your mother told you?"

"Only that I must show him respect."

Amma nodded. "That would be wise, sprigget, as well as proper." She stared out to sea and I fiddled with a cockleshell.

"Where did Vigut come from?" I asked presently.

Amma sighed. "He came from Birsay, where both your parents grew up. Your mother was beautiful then, as she is now. My son, your father, loved her. So did Vigut. But we were rich and he was poor, so your mother's people gave her to us. Vigut never forgot. That will be why he came."

"Which one did my mother want?"

"She wanted Vigut."

I broke my cockleshell in two and threw it out into the water. I had loved my father. I wished very much that my mother had loved him too.

"I don't like Vigut," I said. "He smells of the bear's fat that he rubs in his beard. I don't want him in our house. Or on our farm. Or by my mother's side at night."

"She wants him there, sprigget. And he wants to be there. In such a situation, a wise child will take care. You are not good at that. Now you must learn."

"Amma," I asked, "do you believe that my father and my brothers are dead?"

She stared out to where my cockleshell had disappeared. She could not speak at first, so she just nodded. I took her hand; it was the first time I had thought to comfort her.

When we reached the barn we found my mother, Od, and Vigut killing the first of the cows.

We worked all of each day from then until the beasts were safely killed and cured, and snow had fallen deep, and everything was ready for Odin's sacrifice. When Vigut heard where we were going he laughed and said he would come with us. "Sessing's a fine hall, so I've heard," he said. "Too fine for a fool like Finnulf."

"What do you mean?" Amma asked. But Vigut only laughed again and would not say any more.

FOUR

W E LEFT BEFORE it began to grow light. Amma
hung a new amulet around my neck next to
Thor's hammer. It was one she had worn herself for as long
as I could remember. I'd never seen what lay inside the
leather pouch; to look would have weakened its power. But
she had told me that it held the coiled skeleton of a tiny
snake taken unborn from its mother's belly. Amma had it
when she was a girl. The bones might all be ground to dust
by now, but it was her most precious thing. I knew she was
afraid for me.

Od tied a twist of hair pulled from the tail of my father's
horse around my wrist, and said charms over it. He did this,
I think, as much to keep the horse safe as to protect me.
Vigut had said we would take Bor, not his own beast, even
though Od said Bor wasn't strong enough to pull the sledge
on a three days' journey and bring us back again.

Od did not watch us leave. He harnessed Bor to the
sledge, said something quiet into his left ear, patted his

neck, and stumped back inside the barn. He spared one glance for me, and that glance was troubled.

Amma stood at the door and watched us go. Or rather, listened to us, because it was too dark for her to see us once we were out of the yard. But I saw the yellow square of light shining from the open door, with her black silhouette standing quite still in the doorway, until we topped the hill and started down the other side and the fold of the land hid Smolsund from us, and we were alone in the dark.

When the dawn light came up, late and low as it does in winter, I saw that we were floating on a sea of snow. I'd never left Smolsund before. I'd looked across the land and out over the sea and into water and through sky, but I'd never left our fields and house and barn and beach before.

My mother knew the way. For that matter so did Bor; he'd made the journey every year since first my father had him. It took three days if all went well. You followed the coastline for the first day, then turned east across the long headland, picked up the curve of the coast again on the other side, and followed it for one more day.

There was little to fear from pirates, my mother said, because the land was not rich enough to draw them. Vigut laughed but would not tell her why. Cold was our danger, Mother said, and the gray wolves who come with it, following the snow down from the hills to search for meat along the coastal lands. We had a spear each in case they came. Mine was my brother's. Vigut had his sword and shield and an axe as well, and my mother had a knife.

We had heavy furs to keep us safe from the cold, and a thick woven rug to throw over Bor, as well as a sack of oats to feed him with, and dried meat and bread and beer for us. My mother had told me how it would be. At midday we would stop to eat, and when night was near we would begin to look for shelter. There were no farms between our own and Sessing to give us fire and shelter. But there were woods for the first night and a cave my mother knew for the second.

The long runners of the sledge hissed. Bor's four hooves pushed into the hard snow with a sound like stiff cloth crumpling. When I shut my eyes, the sound went around and around like the beat of poetry. When the going was easy, Vigut made him trot or canter until his warm steam filled our lungs, and flecks of foam blew back on us, and the snow showered up.

"Don't make him work so hard," my mother said to Vigut. "He's got to get us there and back again." Vigut said nothing but he let Bor walk again. The snow balled under his hooves so that he walked on stilts. When there was enough of it, it fell from his hoof. Sometimes, if he was trotting, it flew back and hit us.

Mother sat in front under the great fur rug with Vigut. They leaned in close to one another and talked; I could not hear what they were saying. My mother laughed a lot and so did Vigut. When his long hair blew across her cheek she did not brush it away.

I sat behind, alone.

FIVE

B Y EARLY AFTERNOON the light began to be sucked down into the red mouth of the west. Clouds full of snow lay close over the land like cream on a milk pan. Ahead, between Bor's ears, a low line of trees darkened the horizon.

"Those are the woods we must find shelter in tonight," my mother said to Vigut, pointing.

Vigut laughed and shook Bor's reins. "Your bag of bones won't bring us there by nightfall."

"Make him go faster then!"

"If I do that, he may not last the journey."

"There is no shelter between here and there. If we're caught in the open, he won't last the night. Neither will we."

"Don't fret. We'll find a dip or hollow, some shelter behind rocks maybe, before the dark comes down."

My mother shrugged. Vigut jumped down off the sledge, slapped Bor, and took his bridle. "Your daughter can walk too," he said over his shoulder. "It will lighten the load."

I glanced at my mother. She nodded and I hopped off

into the snow. I had to walk fast, even to keep pace with Bor's slow plod—I'm short, and sank a small way into the snow at each step.

After a mile or two we found ourselves slipping and sliding down into a valley. Vigut pulled Bor to a halt and looked around. The light was going fast; what little there was left seemed to shine out of the ground. The crimson sunset faded to the color of a hen's egg and hung like a soft stain where home lay, behind us.

Vigut was cheerful. He enjoyed adversity. He looked all around, whistling a little through his broken white teeth, then pulled Bor's bridle and led us farther down into the hollow. At the bottom of the little valley a huddle of gray rocks blocked what must have been the path of a small stream in summer. A polish of ice spilled around the rocks, showing where the stream would run and bubble when the spring thaw came. Three hawthorn trees twisted around the rocks. Vigut led Bor in under their branches. My mother scrambled down, stamping her feet, and began to pull firewood off the sledge.

"Set the fire, Astrid," Vigut said. "Make it there between the rocks. Ran, unharness the bone bag. Rub him down, then feed him. Melt snow for him to drink when the fire's hot."

While my mother built the fire, took out her flint, lit the dry moss, and blew on it to make it catch, I twisted up a pinch of straw from the bottom of the sledge and rubbed Bor's wet hide, around and around the way Od did it, to make his blood tingle so he wouldn't chill while the sweat dried on him. It warmed me too and comforted us both. He was afraid out in the open with the darkness closing in around the small glow of our fire.

When he was well warmed I dragged the heavy rug out of the sledge and threw it over him, fastening it with rope around his belly and over his shoulders. Then I tipped oats from the sack onto the ground and let him start his supper. His gentle eyes gleamed like water in the fire flicker, and the crunch and grind of his teeth were pleasant in the night. Mother was warming something on the fire for us. Vigut had scrambled up onto the tallest rock. I doubt he could see much. I expect he was listening.

My mother took the first watch. Vigut told her to keep the fire alight and wake him when she had fed it five times. "Only enough to keep it burning, mind," he said. "It's there to guard us, not to keep us warm. If the horse shows signs of fear, wake me. Ran, you will take the last watch, after me."

He wrapped himself in his fur cloak and lay down on the sledge. I took mine, pulled it around me and up over my head, and lay down as far from Vigut as I could. I pulled my knees up toward my chin and tried not to shiver. I could hear my mother scrambling up onto the rocks and settling herself down to her watch, and I peeped up at her. The stars above her head looked so big and bright it seemed as though I'd hear them singing if I listened long enough. Perhaps she would have loved me as she loved my brothers if only I had looked like her instead of like my father.

The next thing I knew, Vigut's face was close to mine and I could smell the bear's fat in his beard. The firelight shone bright in his eyes as he slid his hand under my cover to pinch me awake.

"Your watch, Eaglebeak," he said. "Or do you mean to sleep all night and let the wolves come in on us?"

"Are they coming?" I asked, sitting bolt upright. "Have you heard them?" Vigut laughed quietly.

"Not yet. But if you shut your eyes before the dawn, they will come creeping on their hungry gray bellies and pull you off the rock. And if *they* don't, I will. I have seen to the fire. Don't let it out."

I scrambled up onto the rock with my cloak around me, hating Vigut. I sat and stared at the blank wall of darkness that enclosed me. Gradually it softened and absorbed my gaze until I could see the outline of the rocks and, below them, the hawthorn trees that leaned and wobbled, lit momentarily by a flame.

Bor moved his weight from hoof to hoof and mumbled oats. Vigut lay down beside my mother on the sledge. She turned her face to his and smiled in her sleep.

There wasn't much to listen to, only the quiet night sounds of our camp. Fire-crackle. Hoof-stamp. Snore. The wind flying over the snow-bedded hills. Sometimes the pulse of my own blood, loud in my ear. Bor couldn't seem to settle. I called down softly to him every now and then, and he'd quiet for a while, but he'd soon start fidgeting again and tugging on his rope.

Presently I heard him snort. I stood up and gripped my spear hard in both hands. I tried to peel back the darkness but I could neither see nor hear what frightened him.

Unquiet spirits possibly. Perhaps my father walked the night. He would be angry to find my mother sleeping in Vigut's arms. I wondered what a drowned man looked like.

Bor put his head back suddenly and neighed. Vigut was up with his sword in his hand before the steam had cleared the air by the horse's nose. Mother jumped from under her covering of furs, grabbed wood, and threw it on the fire. Vigut shouted up to ask me what I'd seen.

"Nothing," I said. "It's still too dark. Maybe Bor was dreaming."

Vigut frowned. "Maybe," he said. "In the morning, when it is light, we will find out if there was something that you should have seen. For now, get down and tend the fire. Take my axe and cut wood from the thorn trees. We may need more before dawn."

I took his axe from the sledge and cut into the living trees, chopping and slashing till I had a bundle as big as the one we'd brought from home. I wondered what Vigut would do if morning showed I had not kept a proper watch.

Bor was calm now, drowsing and dozing as a tired horse will. Mother sat buried in furs. The firelight warmed her hair to gold. Now and then she looked up to where Vigut stood, spear in hand, still as a stone except for where the wind whipped his hair out from under his hat and blew it out across his shoulders.

Gradually the light dispelled the dark. Snow shone and the fire grew pale. I stood up, feet frozen, and hobbled to the sledge to fetch Bor's morning feed. Mother pushed a stale loaf into the warm ashes to heat. Vigut stretched and climbed down from the rock to stroll out across the snow.

"Wolves, a small pack," he said when he returned. "No more than nine or ten. But if they had been hungry, they could have taken Bor." He turned to my mother. "If she sleeps on watch again I shall beat her."

SIX

ALL THAT DAY we pushed Bor along as hard as we dared. We got down from the sledge and walked up every long hill. We ate our midday meal on the move, with Bor taking his oats from a nosebag, stopping only to drink when we found a little stream that ran too fast to freeze. We looked back often. There was no sign of anything following us. But you never do see wolves until they want you to.

"We've surely left them behind," my mother said. But Vigut shook his head.

"Last night they would have known the horse could fight them off. Tonight they will be hungrier, and the bone bag will be weaker. Wolves know such things. They want him."

We were in under the trees by afternoon, and by early evening we had found the cave. It was formed by a fist of rocks buried in the side of a hill. Vigut went in first with his sword drawn to see if it was empty. Mother and I unhitched Bor from the sledge and followed, pulling the horse behind us up the steep bank that formed the doorstep.

Bor did not like the cave. Neither did I. You could tell by its smell that we were not the first travelers of the winter to seek shelter there. Smoke had blackened the high stone ceiling, and a little pile of bones showed where someone had eaten. My mother pushed the bones away into a corner, then laid and lit a fresh fire. I took Bor's harness off and fed him. Mother gave me the leather bucket and told me to fill it with snow and set it near the fire.

Vigut fetched all our furs and food off the sledge and piled them in the cave. He gave me his axe and sent me out to cut more wood.

"Stay near the cave," my mother said. "I don't want to have to look for you."

Tall trees crowded close against the cave mouth. Their bark looked old and cold as stone in the twilight, and the wind lamented through their sharp, dark needles. I could not bring myself to chop at them with Vigut's axe, fearing to anger their spirits. On the far side of a frozen thread of water, a giant had come crashing down in some old gale, gouging out scars in the soft moss, bursting its round brown branches open as it hit the icy ground. I bent and cut, bent and cut, piling up firewood as fast as I could go. My mother came out of the cave, peered into the shadows for me, hurried over, and began to carry the wood into the cave.

Presently, the sledge emptied, Vigut took the axe from me and began to sever the big branches from the fallen trunk. When the pile of firewood at the back of the cave was as tall as my shoulders, Vigut told us to go outside once more if we needed to before the night. After that, he built the branches up into a rough stockade across the cave mouth.

I set a loaf beside the fire and put snow into a pot with salt meat, onion, and dried peas. Mother poured beer into a cup and took it to Vigut. When he had drunk she filled it again for herself and then for me. Its sour tang quenched my thirst and the barley taste of it took away my tiredness.

We built the fire up high, which drove Bor snorting to the back of the cave. I leaned into the pile of furs, spooning up my meat broth, listening to the crackle of the fire, to old Bor's restless stamp, and to my mother singing softly. I felt warm and comfortable for the first time since leaving home.

It felt like deep night when the wolves came. Bor woke me, stamping and snorting in the back of the cave, and I could hear the soft, sing-song whine of their hunger from out beyond the firelight. I jumped up with my spear in my hand. Mother was throwing branches on the fire. Vigut stood a little way in from the cave mouth, sword in one hand, spear in the other.

The stockade shivered as if the wood still grew on living trees bent in the wind. Vigut yelled and struck with his spear, jabbing down through the laced branches. A scream answered his yell and his spear came back bloody.

Everything went silent for a moment. Then a hole appeared between the branches. A gray muzzle pushed through the gap, worrying and tugging to enlarge it. Vigut struck again and it vanished, howling. Then the whole stockade shook violently and five wolves pushed through at once, heads low, eyes intent, lips lifted over yellow fangs. Vigut had speared their leader in the chest. Blood soaked its pelt and dripped onto the snow but it came snarling on, its mate beside it with Vigut's gash open across her snout. The

32

rest hung back a second; then they were on us and the stink of wet wolf filled the cave.

Vigut stabbed the leader with his sword, letting out its lifeblood quickly, but the others poured past, backing Bor against the stone wall of the cave, jostling just out of range of his hooves. I moved my hands down the haft of my spear and ran to my mother. Her spear lay on the ground, and the leader's mate had her by the shoulder. It swung its head from side to side like a dog with a rabbit, pulling her down onto her knees, waiting to shift its grip to her throat and finish her.

I pushed my spear hard into the gray wolf's side. It let my mother go and turned on me. I screamed for Vigut, who took its life with one sharp thrust. He pushed it off his sword and leaped toward Bor. I could not free my spear from the wolf's side so I snatched up Vigut's axe and ran to join him. No need. Of the five who'd ringed Bor, snarling, one was dead and one was dying and the other three were running yelping out across the snow.

My mother did not make a sound while I washed her wounds. She held on to Vigut's hand with her good hand and clenched her teeth. The muscles of her shoulder and her upper arm were torn and she had lost a lot of blood. I bandaged her as gently as I could with my own linen shift. Then I folded Amma's snake-bone amulet into the bandage so that its power would heal her, and I begged her not to die. I took the mead we'd brought for Odin's sacrifice and helped her drink, to take away the sharpest of her pain, holding the cup to her mouth, coaxing sips down her, pleading with her to swallow. I wrapped her in furs, piling them all around her, and chafed her feet and held her hands, but still she shook, whether from cold or shock I did not know. Her apple face was white as bone, her dark eyes big and empty.

When finally she lay still, I got up and went to comfort Bor. He was still afraid, although the wolves had not marked him. I loved my father's horse, but I wished the wolves had sunk their teeth into his hide instead of tearing at my mother's shoulder. Still, I patted him and soothed him, and that soothed me. Then I prayed, speaking quietly so that Vigut would think I was talking to Bor.

"I'm asking you, Freya, because you look after women. And you, Odin Allfather, because you are the most powerful of all the gods. Keep her alive and make her better."

When I went back to my mother, she was asking for Vigut. He was by the stockade, spear in one hand, sword in the other. He had cleaned them both and thrown the bodies out. "I'll watch," I told him. "She wants you."

He nodded and gave me my spear. Then he went back and kneeled beside my mother with his arms around her. I looked away. She wanted him, not me.

SEVEN

WE TOOK MY MOTHER on to Sessing because
it was too far to take her home. She lay in the
sledge with her eyes shut. She drew in her breath each
time a movement jolted her shoulder but gave no other
sign of the pain she must have felt. We changed her
dressings twice during the day. Both times she bled right
through them.

Vigut carried her straight inside the hall when we
arrived, leaving me to see to Bor and the sledge. Sessing is a
rich place, far finer than Smolsund. Even their barns and
outhouses are handsome. A huge tree grew outside their
yard, taller than any I had seen. I passed in under an archway, leading Bor into a paved place enclosed by outbuild-
ings and lit with torches. Two slaves came up and took him
from me. "Rub him down well," I said. "He's tired."

In these fine surroundings, I felt ashamed of Bor. His big
old head hung by his knees and his flat flanks heaved.
Sweat matted his coarse coat and he was marked with
Vigut's whip.

"His oats are on the sledge. I shall come back later to see that all is well," I added, trying to sound like someone to be feared. I took the things I thought Mother would want and went to look for cousin Ristil.

The carving inside the hall was wonderful. Dragons writhed across the polished roof posts. Great shields hung around the walls on wooden paneling; spears leaned in every corner; swords and battle-axes gleamed. Slaves and servants came and went, laying out food and drink. High in the great seat, closest to the fire, sat Finnulf, who owned Sessing, with his wife Thorvi beside him, and guests from other farmsteads around them.

We were the last to come. I blinked in the smoke and noise, and looked around me, feeling my face redden. I had never been among so many people. I wanted to run out to the barn, tell Bor that I was sorry, and spend the night beside him in the straw. I had not then met my cousin, Ristil, and would have to ask for her by name. My mother was nowhere to be seen.

Vigut was standing by the table, drinking from a horn of mead. I saw his eyes over the rim of it, following the best looking of the servant women. I went and stood beside him, waiting to ask him where my mother was. When he had finished drinking, he called the servant over and told her to refill the horn. Then he looked down at me. The mead was working fast on him; he did not try to hide his dislike of me. "She's in the women's room," he said eventually.

I didn't understand. At home we have one room, and it belongs to everyone. The servant brought the horn back full and gave it to him.

"Is this Ran?" she asked, and Vigut nodded. "She's like her father, isn't she? I'll take her to her mother," she said. Vigut scowled, but the servant woman smiled at me and put her hand on my shoulder, pushing me gently in front of her between the throng of guests to where a thick curtain of horsehide hung across a doorway. We pushed past it, entering a smaller room that was darker, cooler, and less fouled with smoke than the hall. Big looms stood around the walls. My mother lay on a wide bench in the middle, cushioned on furs and wrapped around with woollen blankets.

"This is the weaving room," the woman said. "And I'm your cousin, Ristil. We laid your mother here to rest. Gullveig has been sent for."

I went across and crouched beside my mother, stroking her good hand. Her face was white and fragile as a bird's egg. Her breathing hardly lifted the rugs that wrapped her. Ristil laid her hand on my mother's forehead. "Your mother is cold," she said. "I will light a fire for her."

"Is my mother going to die?" I asked.

"She has lost more blood than she can spare. Stay with her, while I find you meat and drink."

EIGHT

I MUST HAVE CLOSED my eyes and slept, though only for a moment. When I woke up a crooked woman stood by my mother. The glimmer from her downcast eyes made me think of Ran, my namesake, whose eyes have been washed and washed under the sea. A tremor shook her body, making her head wobble. Bones and green touchwood hung from her belt, and an old leather pouch from which she took a little vial, her hands jerking and fumbling with the stopper. She dripped something between my mother's lips, leaned close to her and listened to her chest, sniffing her like a dog. She straightened as much as she was able, and her shadow fluttered up the wall behind her. She threw a pinch of dust onto the fire, causing smoke to coil up, honey-slow, into the thick brown thatch.

I coughed then, and Gullveig looked at me. Everything about her was nodding and trembling in perpetual motion except her still, cold eyes. I think she would have spoken to me but Ristil came to the door, carrying a bowl of food. She lifted her chin to tell me to follow her, and I stepped out into the bright, noisy hall.

I crossed the fore and middle fingers of both hands and laid them over one another, like little goat's horns, to ward off evil. "Gullveig's a witch," I said. "I will stay with my mother."

"You will stay in the hall," Ristil told me. "Gullveig works alone."

"But my mother may want me," I pleaded. I could not say, "But I want my mother."

"You do not like old Gullveig. Nobody does. But we send for her fast enough when we need her. When sickness strikes or crops won't grow. When we miscarry or love won't go the way we want it to, when wounds won't heal or the dead trouble the living, we send for Gullveig."

"And does she mend things?"

Ristil nodded. "She is powerful. Be patient. Do what is best for your mother and stay here. When Gullveig has finished, I'll call you."

I nodded and sat where she told me with the bowl of food in front of me, though I could not eat. I knew that I must trust her.

I had not heard a harp before that night in Finnulf's hall, only Od's whistle. The first chord the singer struck flew up and down my spine like bees. I caught only a fragment of the words, after the first "Hear Thou." He sang *The Prophecy*, which tells about the end of this world and the beginning of the next:

Land sinks beneath the sea
the sun dims
from the sky
fall the fair bright stars

I have heard *The Prophecy* sung many times since then, but never quite like that.

NINE

THE SINGER'S HAIR was shiny and smooth, like gold wire smelted by dwarves under the mountains. It was long, but its weight did not stop it curling and twisting around his face like the tendrils of a vine. I could not see his eyes while he was playing. He seemed to watch his own hands on the harp. When he looked up, I saw that he was blind.

Hearing him sing, I forgot my mother. I forgot Gullveig and Ristil and Vigut, roaring around the hall now, drunk and growing drunker. I forgot I was in Sessing, or anywhere, except with him. It was not until the noise of shouting stopped him singing that I remembered where I was and looked around the torch-lit hall. The air was curdled with wood smoke. Some of the men had drunk themselves to sleep. There was still meat on the long table, and bowls of mead and beer. Slaves stood by the walls, looking as blank as only slaves can. Finnulf was on his feet, with Thorvi, his wife, beside him.

I looked where they were looking, and saw Vigut with his back to me, shaking something. A long scream sucked the air out of the hall. Two of Finnulf's sons jumped up and pulled Vigut away. Gullveig fell from him, her shaking, quaking dance made wilder by her terror as she laid a long and powerful curse upon him. I knew what Vigut's anger meant, and Gullveig's fear. I was up and across the hall and running to my mother in the weaving room before the witch's scream had faded from the silent hall.

My mother lay on the wide bench, still wrapped around with furs and blankets. Her hair shone in the firelight. Her eyes were shut, and her long eyelashes cast sharp, dark shadows on her cheeks. I was too late to say good-bye to her. I could not kiss that cold, dead face.

Amma had all my kisses when I was a child; my mother never wanted them. Amma loved me and comforted me when my mother beat me. Now that my mother was dead, her not loving me could never be put right.

Later, I saw how the blood had run where Gullveig had cut the bandage from her shoulder. But at first, and for some time, I saw only her face. The flesh looked solid, carved from yellow bone, the features sharp and clear and empty.

Vigut blundered in behind me sobbing, pushed me away, and began to kiss her face. The room filled with women—Thorvi, guests, maids, slaves. They shooed Vigut away, brought water to wash my mother with, and a clean robe. I wanted them to stop. She was my mother. This was the last of my time with her. I did not want it crowded out by strangers.

She did not think much of me when she was alive. Her sons were all her joy. I remember, when I was a little girl, sitting on Amma's knee, watching and listening while my mother told them stories. She told them about Odin's sacred ravens, whose names mean Thought and Memory. She told them about Sleipnir, Odin's eight-legged horse, and Gungnir, his magic spear. She told them about Jormungand, the snake who hugs the world down in the deep, encircling ocean, and Garm, the guardian of the gates of Hel. I loved her stories, but they were not for me.

Amma would hug me, and tell me that I was her little queen, her only granddaughter, her blessing and delight. And so I was. But I wanted my mother to love me too. Now she never would. Now her spirit would dive down through the cold green waters of the deep salt sea to Ran's great hall, dark on the ocean floor. There she would search for her lost sons and, finding them, add to the volume of the sea her own salt tears of happiness.

TEN

"KISS YOUR MOTHER," Ristil said, pushing me toward her. I shook my head. "You must," she whispered. "It's expected." So I did it, and bending, smelled the blood that soaked her bandages.

The women took her robe off carefully and dressed her in a new shift, because her old one was all stained and ragged. They gently unwound the dark red strips of bandages from around her shoulder, laying bare the marks of the wolf in her flesh. Her whole shoulder, her upper arm, her chest, were dark and swollen with disease. When the last wet coil of bandage fell away, Amma's little snake-bone amulet, which I had tucked into the folds, dropped onto the floor. One of the women stooped to pick it up. It fell into two halves in her hand and there, curled around like a sliver of new moon, lay the fine white skeleton of the tiny snake.

The woman turned as white as bone herself and laid it down, rubbing her hands on her dress, crossing her fingers to avert evil. Thorvi looked at the little twist of bone and sent for Gullveig.

They brought her in, a slave on each side of her—none of the free women would go near her. She was spitting venom, terrified and angry. A piece of cloth covered her mouth to prevent her from laying curses.

"What is it, Gullveig?" Thorvi asked, taking the cloth away. The old witch shook her head. "Tell us. Otherwise we'll make you."

Thorvi picked a burning log out of the fire. She was not a cruel woman. I could see that by looking at her face. There was neither pleasure nor excitement there. But she knew what was due to a guest who had been murdered by magic under her own roof. Gullveig shook her head, and Thorvi held the burning wood against her wrinkled forearm.

I have never been able to stomach pain, neither my own nor other people's. I don't like slaughtering the beasts, particularly pigs, which scream, although I know it must be done. When my father beat Od, I'd run away and hide, and Amma wouldn't find me until evening. Gullveig had hardly opened her mouth to start yelling before I'd slipped from Ristil's arms and pushed the burning log away. Thorvi raised both her eyebrows. It was not my place to interfere, and anyway, I should have been the first to demand Gullveig's death by fire, as my mother's daughter.

"The snake is mine," I said. "My grandmother gave it to me, in an amulet, to keep me safe on my journey. When my mother was wounded, I tucked it into the bandage to stop her bleeding. I thought it would heal her wound."

While I was speaking, the men came crowding into our room from the hall. They had heard Gullveig yelling and had come to watch the fun. Vigut was at the front. As I finished speaking and looked up, I caught him staring at me. His face was heavy and red with wine and weeping, and his eyes were bloodshot.

"She put it there!" he spat. "The little bitch. I saw her do it, and she admits it freely! She was muttering magic while she did it. She's a cold fish like her namesake. She never loved her mother. She was her grandma's suckling, made much of when she wanted beating. Her father was a weak man. Well, I will set that right with her."

Gullveig nodded and Vigut slipped his belt off, but Finnulf came up behind him and caught his hand before he had a chance to raise it. "There'll be no beating here unless I order it," he said. Two of his sons placed themselves on either side of Vigut and marched him back into the hall. Thorvi, meanwhile, was looking at me less than warmly.

"You've lost your mother, child," she said. "No doubt you are distressed." Her cool eyes searched my face but evidently found no signs of sorrow there. To tell the truth, it wasn't sorrow that I felt, so much as anger. Anger at my mother for being dead now when I needed her. Anger that she had loved my brothers without loving me. Anger that now I'd never hear her say that she was sorry. Anger that she had loved Vigut, who called my father a weak man and threatened to beat me in front of everybody.

Gullveig pointed a bony finger at me and began to whine. "She's the one. She has powerful magic. She crossed my healing spells. She drew the blood from her poor mother's veins. Most likely it was she who called up the wolves. We are all in danger, while she lives."

Ristil spoke from behind my back. "She was quick enough to put herself in danger when you were yelling, Gullveig."

It was only then, I think, that I understood how bad things were for me.

"Take Gullveig to the barn," Thorvi told the slaves who held her. "And keep her there till morning."

They took the witch away, and you could not have said which of them was more afraid—the slaves of the coming night in the barn with Gullveig, or Gullveig of the morning.

Thorvi turned to Ristil, who still stood close behind me with one hand resting on my shoulder. "This child is kin to you, Ristil," she said. "Stay with her. She shall pass a last night in her mother's company. Tomorrow will be soon enough to do what must be done."

Everyone left the room then, like water from a sieve, and I began to cry. Ristil banked up the fire. I wiped my nose on the sleeve of my gown and went to stand beside my mother. I put my hand out to touch her face, but drew it back at once. I had not known that she would feel so dead. I cried, shivering and shaking, until my eyes stung and my throat burned and my face was swollen and my shoulders ached, because I would never be my mother's lovely daughter, light of her life or apple of her eye. Now I would always be sour Ran, Amma's pet, the one who lived when those who were more precious died.

Presently Ristil drew the covers up over my mother's face and told me to lie down, and I slept, lying on a bearskin by the fire.

ELEVEN

RISTIL WOKE ME before dawn. I felt as if I hadn't slept at all, then wondered how I could have, with my mother's body lying cold upon the bench beside me.

"Drink this," Ristil said, putting a bowl of hot milk in my hands. I shook my head and closed my eyes. "Drink it," she said. "We must make plans. Tomorrow's nearly here. It must not start before we're ready for it."

"What will they do?" I asked. "Will they put me to the test, to see if I'm lying about the amulet? I cannot bear pain, Ristil."

"I think they will. And you must bear it. It need not be as dreadful as you think. I can get powerful medicine for you, Ran, to numb the pain. And if you're quick, the injury will be slight."

Mostly, the test is boiling water. They fill a vat with it and drop stones in. The woman who's accused of lying picks them out. Then her hands are bandaged. They take the bandages off three days later. Clean wounds mean she told the truth. Infection means she lied. I had never seen it done, but I knew about it.

"I cannot, Ristil. You know I did not kill my mother. Tell them, Ristil. Tell them I told the truth. The amulet was Amma's, and there was no evil in it."

"They will not listen to me, Ran. You know they will not. I will be with you. You will not be alone."

I sat in the dark room beside my mother's body, praying to those who spin our destinies and fates, but without much hope. After a while I knew what I must do. I would not suffer agony in Sessing's hot hall among a crowd of enemies. I heard the dogs begin to twitch and snuffle in the hall, and stood up.

"Ristil," I lied, "I'm hungry. Will you fetch me some bread?"

"Gladly," she said. "I'll bring you soup as well."

I took my good fur cloak and grabbed a short spear from the wall. I said good-bye to my mother and crept out into the yard. The torches had long since burned out, the fire had dwindled to nothing, and the night was still and black as basalt. The stars were brighter than I'd ever seen them, glittering and dancing in the sable sky. I hurried out under the archway; the cold wind caught me and took my breath away. Dawn licked a brown edge to the east.

The sun would rise, and Skoll, the wolf who chases him across the sky, would gallop after him. At Ragnarok, when the world ends, Skoll will swallow him, and everyone will die. But not me, and not here, I thought. I will go back to Amma, who loves me. Somehow, I'll find my way back to her. As soon as the sun comes up I'll know which way to walk. A little snow will cover my footsteps. All I need is time.

It was evening when Vigut caught me and brought me back to Sessing. No doubt he could have found me earlier if he'd wanted to, but he had stayed to see the end of Gullveig. She had confessed to murdering my mother with the snake, and died according to the law, all in the space of one short day. I would not have wished such suffering on anyone. But I had been so much afraid of the test, and of the death I would have died if my hands had blistered, that I could not help rejoicing silently that it was she, not me, who died.

"That old hag did not kill your mother," Vigut said, throwing me up onto his horse.

"She said she did. You told me that she said she did."

"She would have said anything by then."

"She was a witch. Everybody knows that."

I knew wolves, not magic, had killed my mother. But Gullveig was dead. They couldn't hurt her any more. So long as they believed in her guilt, I was safe.

Thorvi greeted me kindly and sat me down beside the fire to eat. "What were you thinking of, Ran?" she asked. "You must have known that you were innocent. The test would have told us so if Gullveig had not. You will see your grandmother soon enough. It's lucky Vigut cared enough to go after you, or you would surely have died in the snow."

Ristil brought my supper, her face showing only pleasure at my safe return and not a trace of anger that I'd run. She rubbed my feet with goose fat because the snow had chapped them, and made me drink foul things to ward off fever. We did not speak of Gullveig.

"Your mother's funeral will be tomorrow," Ristil said. "Toki, the blind musician, will sing for her. We'll sacrifice. She'll have the honors that are due to her. You must play your part too and make a speech. Tonight you can rest in my room."

Ristil's two boys, Hal and Hold, lay snoring softly on a pallet, rolled together in one rug. Hal, the elder, clutched a tiny wooden longboat to his chest, a gift his father made him from a twist of firewood and a snippet of cloth. Hold was still a baby, creased and secret in his sleep, his round cheek pressed against his brother's ear.

I lay beside the children, listening to their snores and snuffles. Hal dropped his boat and felt around for it, eyes shut. I picked it up and tucked it back into his palm. Hold began to smack his lips, dreaming no doubt of Ristil's milky breasts. He tried to nibble at his brother's ear, but Hal pushed him away.

I leaned up on one elbow, watching them. Had my brothers been so sweet when they were little? And did our mother lean over their sleeping faces, watching dreams come and go behind their eyelids, as I now leaned, watching Ristil's boys?

TWELVE

RISTIL CALLED ME early, and we went into the women's room, which had begun to smell different. My mother lay on the bench with her waxy, white flesh washed clean of blood and dirt, her dark eyes closed and sunken, her pale hair hidden by a headcloth, limbs straight and still. What lay there looked like her, but was not her, and I felt a sort of crawling horror. I would not have been surprised to see her hands move, or one eye flicker open.

Vigut came in with four exhausted, muddy slaves behind him. He looked at her face and looked away, and I could tell he was afraid too. "Cover your mother's face," he snapped. "Are you a halfwit? Don't you know we're going to bury her?"

I took the very edges of her headcloth and drew them over her silent, empty face. Tears stung my eyes, trickled down my cheeks, and dripped off my chin. Risitl pushed a soft fold of cloth into my hand. I wiped my eyes and then my nose and stared down stupidly at my mother's still hands until Ristil gently pulled me back. I knew then that I loved her, even though she had never loved me.

The slaves picked up the bench, one to each corner, and carried it outside into the yard. They waited while another slave led Bor out of the barn, Finnulf following with a sharp knife in his hand. I had not known Bor was to be my mother's sacrifice.

We trailed out of the yard, under the stone arch, into a flurry of falling snow. The grave had been dug during the night. Finnulf lifted my mother off the bench and laid her down in it.

Someone, Ristil perhaps, had polished her fine brooches, and they shone at her breast. Her silver arm ring glimmered against the skin of her arm. The cloth I'd pulled across her face fell back, and for a moment she looked as though she'd just lain down to rest. A little snow powdered her forehead, but it did not melt.

They led Bor up, snorting and blowing in the early morning cold, roped his legs, and threw him down on his side. Finnulf cut Bor's throat, and he kicked and struggled while his blood soaked out onto the snow. I did not think about my father, whose horse he was, until it was finished. Then I cried again and Ristil put her arms around me. The slaves hauled Bor's hulk over toward my mother's feet. They covered her and Bor with earth, forming a broad mound by the time they'd finished. We stood and watched until they were done, then went back to the hall, leaving my mother alone with Bor under the earth.

There was food indoors, and fire, and drink, which Vigut started on at once.

Toki began a praise song for my mother. He told how she had grown up on the Brough of Birsay, where her father was a wealthy farmer. How he died in a raid, and how his daughter married, and how she had made the voyage to the northwest homelands, close by Sessing, with her husband and his people. He told how my father and my brothers had gone to live with Ran under the ocean, and how my mother, now, had plunged below the waves in spirit to be with them, leaving me and my grandmother behind. It was a good enough song, considering that he did not know us.

Finnulf and Thorvi spoke, and then it was my turn. I stood up, and looked at Thorvi's face. She smiled at me; I cleared my throat and started. Ristil had told me what to say. I thanked Finnulf and Thorvi for asking us to their fine hall to celebrate the sacrifices. I told them I was sorry we had delayed Allfather's celebration, and praised their hospitality again. A supplicant says thank-you often. I said that my mother had been a brave and honest woman, a loyal wife, a fine farmer, and a kind mother. Those are the things you have to say, Ristil had told me. I ended by praising Finnulf and Thorvi for honoring my mother with so fine a funeral, and asking if I might repay them in some small way by staying on at Sessing till the spring, doing such work as Thorvi should see fit to give me.

This last was Ristil's idea. "You cannot travel back with Vigut, that's for sure," she said. "Even the gods could not protect you from a man like that. He'd certainly rape you and probably sell you afterward. You must stay here till the spring. All kinds of people will be on the road again by then; we'll find you a safe escort easily.

Your grandmother will think you're dead, but that cannot be helped."

I slept that night in Risitl's room again. The hall was quiet; everyone was tired. Only the slaves still labored, cleaning and cooking in preparation for Allfather's celebrations. Brokk was to be the master of ceremonies, Ristil told me.

Brokk lived alone beside the sea, half a day's walk from Sessing. Half a day for a man, but a day's walk for Brokk, who was a dwarf. I had never seen a dwarf, though Amma had told me stories of them. Brokk was shorter than me, Ristil said, but broad and muscled as any man, and famous for his temper.

"He's a cruel man," she said, "but whether his cruelty comes of his calling, or whether it's grown because of the cruel way fate dealt with him, making him small and tormenting him with aches and pains, I wouldn't know."

"What is his calling?" I asked.

"Allfather must have his sacrifices, and Brokk's the one who chooses them. That's what I think, anyway, though he says differently."

"What does he say?"

"He says the sacrifice must choose itself."

"Why, though?"

"Our Master of Magic, Odin Allfather, chose himself to be our sacrifice. He learned the wisdom of the dead by dying, and brought it back to share with us. Nine days and nine long nights he hung from the great world tree, riding the gallows horse, with a sharp spear in his side. No comfort and no company came near him. That is why we call

55

him Our Lord of the Gallows. Nine days, nine nights he hung, before death would accept his sacrifice. Nine songs he learned, and eighteen powerful runes. And from them come all knowledge. He paid for them. And every year we must repay him."

"But what does Brokk do, Ristil?"

"Brokk is the one who knows when a person is ready to repay. He looks at them, and he knows. *That one*, he says. Often the person does not know themselves until after Brokk has spoken. Sometimes even then they do not understand, but Brokk gives them medicine to clear their minds. And when they understand, he puts the spear in their side, and the noose under their chin, and sends them to Allfather. Have you never seen it?"

I shook my head.

"It's a great mystery. Only, I do not like it when a child chooses to go."

She said no more, and we were busy then, throwing rushes on the floor, driving the dogs out, roasting meat, fetching firewood from the barn, filling lamps, trimming wicks. I had slipped fast enough from guest to servant. In the middle of it all, Brokk arrived.

He stalked into the hall, leaving a trail of muddy snow behind him. A sack hung on his back. A tattered crow perched on his shoulder, and a thin hound tried to slink in at his heels, but he kicked it back out. His large dark eyes searched all about the hall. Everywhere he looked, people were suddenly busy. Somebody ran to fetch Thorvi and she came striding in, head high and unafraid, and greeted him politely. She brought him to the table and told me, because

I was nearest, to fetch him mead and hot food from the kitchen. She set a slave to pulling off his boots and warming his feet, which were yellow and thick with calluses.

Finnulf came up and bowed politely. "Welcome," he said, "Master of Ceremonies, Magic-maker, Fear-bringer, Servant to Odin Allfather." He slid a gold ring off his little finger and put it on Brokk's thumb. "Make Sessing yours while you are here," he smiled. "Be sure to tell me where you wish to sleep. And who with."

Both men laughed. Brokk picked tidbits from the table and fed them to his bird, whose name was Kraku. His eye meanwhile continued to glance around the hall, and stopped at a young woman who was scrubbing down the tables. Her long red braids kept dangling in her water bucket. She did not notice Brokk watching her. But she shivered all the same and pulled her shawl tight around her shoulders, tucking back her braids.

THIRTEEN

THE CEREMONY BEGAN at sunset. The slaves lit torches all around the walls. Small Brokk may have been, but his presence filled the fire-lit space he moved through. Two polished horns like sickle moons curved out on either side of his pale forehead. His robes were dark, like his eyes, which glittered in the red light. Kraku, the draggled bird, still perched behind his ear.

Brokk carried a spear in his left hand. Very old it looked, the blade worn smooth by countless sacrifices, the haft polished to ebony by a hundred hands before his own. In his right hand he held a coil of rope.

He passed down the length of the hall, a wide space opening up around him as he walked. When he got to the high seat by the fire, he hitched himself up onto the chair they'd set there for him and sat looking down at his hands, not moving.

Finnulf beckoned to the red-haired woman, who came up with a jug and filled Brokk's bowl at arm's length. He emptied it at one swallow and held it out for more. Every one feasted then. Somewhere between sunset and that part of every night when you feel the sun is gone forever, Toki began to sing.

He sang of the creation of the world, when there was only ice and snow in the north, and fire in the south, and between them nothing but Ginnungagap where the eleven rivers fill the emptiness with ice.

He sang of the rivers that flowed out of the north and melted as they reached the south, and of the giant and his cow, who grew out of the melting ice water. He sang of how the cow licked the shape of a man out of the ice, and how the man walked free and found a mate. And how, of their three children, Odin Allfather was the greatest and the best.

He sang of how Odin killed his father and made the world out of his body. His flesh became earth. His bones became mountains. His blood filled oceans. His skull formed the high dome of the sky and Odin blew his father's brains about to make the clouds.

It is a long song and a fine one, and Toki sang it well. When he struck his final chord and the hall fell silent, I felt as though I stood under the very dome of Allfather's father's skull.

Brokk hopped down off his high seat and stood by the fire. He pulled a snakeskin rattle from the folds of his dark robe. Two white bones hung from it on leather thongs. As Brokk twisted it, they tapped against the stretched skin and sent a pattering rhythm out among the shadows. Dogs whined and whimpered. Men and women shifted softly as the patter of Brokk's rattle slowly filled the hall, emptying our hearts of Toki's music, sending its own dark message into every ear, until we felt it tapping in our heads.

Brokk walked among us, twisting and twisting the rattle in his left hand. Every now and then he'd stop and look deeply into one face or another, and each face he looked into grew blank with fear. He walked all around the hall and back to the high table, where Finnulf and Thorvi sat watching. He looked up at Finnulf, and his small left hand grew still. The bones of his rattle faltered and tapped their way to silence.

Finnulf got slowly to his feet. "Do you find no gift here for Allfather, Brokk? Holds my hall no willing sacrifice?"

"Our Lord of the Gallows is angry," Brokk replied, and the silence cracked like cat ice under his deep voice. "You should not have kept him waiting."

"Allfather knows we had a funeral to attend to," Thorvi said. "How could we offer to him with a woman lying dead among us?"

"You should have sent for me to come to Sessing sooner. I judge how best to please Allfather. That is my work."

Nobody else could have spoken to Thorvi like that and gotten away with it.

"What can we do?" asked Finnulf. "What can we give to our Lord of the Gallows to turn his anger into love for us?"

"Bring me a cock and a hen," Brokk said.

A woman ran out to the yard and came back with a sleepy fowl under each arm. Brokk drew a little shining knife from out of his sleeve and slit their throats, spilling blood and feathers down the woman's dress. Then he threw the corpses on the fire, filling the hall with the smell of burning meat and feathers.

He asked for his bowl, drank and drank again, then hopped around the fire watching the birds shrivel in the flames. When they had turned to ash, he lowered his spear and began to turn himself around and around.

When he stopped turning, his spear led him to me.

FOURTEEN

Y OU ARE RIGHT," he said, nodding at me. "You have spoken. The chosen always know." The points of his horns caught the light as they dipped and rose again.

"No, no," I said. "It isn't me."

"Allfather speaks to me," Brokk answered. "Just as he speaks to you. And you must listen. Gullveig died for the sake of a snake but Allfather knows whose fault it was."

A sigh ran around the hall. Odin had chosen.

Someone gripped my arms tightly from behind while Brokk went back to his place at the table. He gave the rope to Finnulf, who took it out into the night. Brokk rummaged in his sack and brought out a bulging leather flask. Even before he made me drink from it, everything seemed to be a long way off, as though I was looking down through a sheet of ice to the dark bottom of the pond at home. Once, when I was a child, I saw a fish frozen into the ice down there, with another fish grasped in its teeth. It seemed to me now that Brokk was the big fish, held in the ice of his own magic, and I the little one, locked in his jaws.

I saw Ristil working her way around the hall, stopping everywhere to refill horns and mugs. She finished up by Toki, touched his hand, whispered, then bent to hear his quiet answer.

Brokk stepped toward me with the spear in one hand and the flask in the other. He came up close and smiled, and the red of the torchlight turned his dark eyes black.

"Come to Brokk, little chicken," he said, but quietly so that only I could hear. Then he pushed the neck of the flask between my teeth and tipped it up, filling my mouth and throat with scalding, burning fire. I choked and spat and swallowed until the flask dangled empty in Brokk's white hand, and sight and sound and smell spun me off my feet and up high somewhere above the roof beams, from where I would look down and watch my going.

Brokk began to twist his snakeskin rattle, and my mind spun and my heart jumped with its patter.

Toki struck a chord on his harp, and the sweet sound of it billowed out across the smoky hall, driving Brokk's darkness out, sending it racing through the door and out into the night. I saw Brokk running with it like a spider, out into the snow, and still he stood over me, the empty flask dangling from one hand. Shape-shifter, I thought. Magician. I saw the torchlight burnishing his spear, and the shadow of the rope writhing like a serpent up into the great tree outside the yard. I saw it raise its head and twist its tail into a noose, while Toki's chord beat like the wings of a swan, and his voice leaped like a silver fish mounting the bright steps of a waterfall to spawn, singing to me of light and life and freedom.

Ristil came down the hall, ignored me, and spoke to Brokk, bending low to whisper in his ear. He nodded, and leaned down to me. Toki's chord fluttered down to earth and lay still among the rushes. Something bright left the hall, and I began to weep.

"It is time, chicken," Brokk said. "This woman says the singer wants to sip from your small cup before you go. He would send greetings to Allfather through your little body. It's his right."

Ristil pulled me up onto my feet. Someone else lifted me up, carried me out into the icy darkness, and dropped me onto the snow. I sank a little into the white, soft feathers of winter, and lay there, floating like a gull on the wind. I saw the stars above my face, bright and white. I heard them drawing breath as they saw me, and I thought that they would sing for me, but they only watched me, quietly, and breathed.

Then I was lifted high. The rope, I thought. I thanked Allfather that I had felt no pain. Then I heard shouting and screaming and all the dogs of Sessing barking, and the hall glowed red behind me. The world lurched, and I spun out across the sky toward my death.

I smelled the hot, salt smell of horse, and knew that Allfather had sent his eight-legged horse to fetch me. I cried, because my journey to Sessing was ending on the gallows tree.

FIFTEEN

I HAVE SEEN SOMETHING of death since then, and I know he does not come so easily in general. Death came hungry to Sessing that night, and went off with stuffed guts, but I was not the feast.

When the foul fumes of the muck Brokk made me drink that night had cleared from my brain, which did not happen till I had voided every last drop of it from my belly, and some time after I thought my skull would burst, I found myself riding a horse with four legs, not eight. And we were going to the coast, not Hel.

It was morning, and in front of me a huge wolfhound wrote paw prints on the crisp white slope of a hillside up ahead. The horse I rode was fine, for all he had only four legs. His coat was light gray, his mane and tail milk white, his eyes shining and deep and knowledgeable, and his name was Kund. Toki, the musician, rode behind me.

I was alive, and not hanging like a bat from the branches of the gallows tree. But I had been offered up to Odin, and it was the right and duty of any person finding me alive to send me to him. If Toki didn't do it, Brokk and half the men of Sessing would. If Toki meant to kill me, why had he waited? And if he didn't mean to, why were we plodding east toward the sea? Along the coast we ran the risk of meeting other travelers. We should be heading west, inland to where the mountains or the woods might give us shelter. My head hurt, and it was all too hard to understand. I looked back along the trail of Kund's hoof prints. Behind us the soft hills folded in on one another like egg white beaten in a bowl. A dark line showed where the far headland and Sessing lay. Between it and us nothing stirred.

"Nobody's coming after us," Toki said.

"Why not?"

"Because most of them are dead. And if you're going to void any more of Brokk's potion, I'd be glad if you'd lean out a little farther than you did before."

"Dead? How?"

I thought of Ristil and her two sons, Hal and Hold. I thought of Thorvi. Finnulf I did not care about, and I hoped, if it was true, that Brokk had been the first to die. A gust of wind blew Toki's red hair into my face. It tickled my neck, and I leaned back against his warmth, which comforted me. I promised myself that I would wash, and in warm water, as soon as I could. At least, I thought, he cannot see me, even if he can smell me. And all the while I thought also of Sessing and of all who lived, and maybe died, there.

"Did you not hear the fighting, Ran?"

"I heard shouting, and screaming, and dogs barking, and

the roar of flames. Before I was lifted up. Before the smell of horse. I thought perhaps that it was in my mind. Was it a raid?"

"It was. And I think your Vigut was expecting it. I heard him curse Finnulf and greet the raiders as I left."

"He's not my Vigut. Is he dead?"

"I didn't stop to find out. Ristil came to me, when Brokk chose you for the sacrifice. She wanted me to run away with you. She said they'd soon forget and choose another sacrifice. I doubt they would have, but the raiders came just as she led me to you. I pulled you up out of the snow and took you to the barn. Kund carried us both away."

Toki slid off Kund's back and walked, his shoulder near my knee. The wolfhound Kon ran back and nosed his hand, then padded on ahead, regular as rainfall. I rode and Toki walked until the dark came down, and it was only when we stopped to shelter for the night that I first wondered how he knew where we were going.

Our shelter was the same cave that my mother took her fatal wound in. I had not even recognized the path, and when I realized where we were I was unwilling to go in, but Toki told me not to be a child.

A little of our wood was left, and I cut more. Toki harnessed Kund up to a fallen tree trunk and told me to make him drag it back into the cave. Then he drove the horse to the back of the cave, which Kund liked no better than Bor had. Toki sent Kon off to hunt for his dinner and ours, and the hound came back, some time after I thought that we had surely lost him, with the back half of a doe dangling from his jaws. He dropped it at Toki's feet and thumped his tail on the cave floor while Toki praised and thanked him.

"He's only brought you half the deer," I said. "Aren't you going to beat him?"

"No," Toki answered. "He feeds himself in order to feed me and I thank him for it. Cut it up and cook it."

I cut and cooked while Toki fetched still more wood. I showed him where the fallen tree lay, and he did not stop until we had enough for half a dozen little fires, which he built and lit all across the cave mouth on top of the log. We had a little wall of fire between ourselves and darkness, and enough wood stacked behind us to feed it until dawn.

"Why are you doing that?" I asked, as Toki lit and blew and settled in the fires.

"Because I'm blind and cannot fight. Would you rather I gave your little body to the wolves, since you withheld it from Allfather?"

I shook my head. It was a long time before I learned not to do that.

"No," he continued, as though he'd seen me. "You are right. Why waste it on them?"

He sang while he made Kund comfortable, and I roasted the meat on sticks over the fire. The wood crackled and the meat spat. Kund blew contentedly into his sack of oats, and Kon grunted, as dogs do when they're happy.

"Is it true what they say about Ran?" he asked presently.

"What do they say?"

"They say she has a stormy temper and a net that catches anything her heart desires."

"That I don't know," I said. "How did you find this place?"

"I am a musician and must move from farm to farm.

Usually I travel in company with other people. In winter, when the roads are empty, I hole up; there are places where I'm welcome and can stay till spring. But when I wish to travel on my own, Kon and Kund lead me."

"How?"

Toki took a leather flask from his sack and pulled the wooden spigot from its neck with his teeth. He held the flask out to me but I shook my head, again. I was very thirsty, but Brokk's flask taught me a bitter lesson.

"Perhaps your silence means you think it's poison, Ran? Or magic medicine to make you think you're riding Odin's eight-legged horse instead of my four-legged Kund? You talk when you're drunk, Ran. Of a fish with a fish in its mouth. And of little furry bees that fly up and down your backbone when you hear the harp."

He drank and held the flask out to me once again. I took it, sniffed it, recognized the smell of barley beer, and drank.

"I wasn't drunk," I said. "Brokk gave me poison."

Toki laughed. "I know." He put his hand on my hand lightly. "I do not think he'll poison anyone again."

I cut a piece of meat for him and stuck it on a stick. "It's hot," I said. "Take care."

When we had eaten all the meat, he gave the bone to Kon. Then he got up, walked over to the burning log, and fed its little fires.

"I doubt there's anything out there that will harm us," he said quietly. "Kon and Kund sound quite peaceful, and I think they would know if there was. But it's possible they followed us from Sessing. Will you sleep first or watch first, Ran?"

"I'll watch first."

"Call me if you need me. We have no weapons other than my knife. Take it and try to keep a stick dipped in the fire."

He rolled himself in a blanket he took from his sack and lay down next to Kon. Soon both of them were sleeping, and I could study Toki to my heart's content. His hair and beard shone softly, and his nose curved a little, like mine, only longer. One of his large hands lay on Kon's shoulder, like a mother's. His feet stuck out of the end of his blanket, one in its leather boot, the other out.

SIXTEEN

I WOKE DEEP IN THE NIGHT, with Toki's hand shaking my shoulder. I had been dreaming about the Fenris wolf from out of Iron Wood. He had a face like Vigut's. Far out among the trees under the moon I heard a wolf's long howl.

"She isn't hunting," Toki said. "There's no danger. I would have let you sleep except that you were crying. Lie down beside the fire. A blind man keeps watch well in the dark."

"Will you know when to feed the fires?" I asked.

"Better than you, Ran, because I shall be awake and will feel when the flames are dying down."

I laughed—ashamed to have fallen asleep. Toki sat down beside me with his rug pulled around us both. I watched the moon float free of the clouds. It lit the soft tops of the pine trees, as though the wood were some great sleeping animal and the trees its pelt.

Far in the distance, framed in the dark curve of the cave mouth, a little hill rose from the woods, silver and smooth.

As I watched, a lone gray wolf crept out across the snow. It made its way to the very center of the hilltop and stood looking at the moon. Presently, it laid back its ears, lifted its muzzle, and let loose into the night a long, lone wail, the very sound of sorrow. It rose and fell and dwindled down to nothing, raising the hair on my head, making Kon shake and shiver.

"She's a singer," Toki said. "Like me."

We sat perfectly still, listening. Up on the snowy hill the wolf seemed to do the same. Soon, from far away, came the reply she longed for—many wolf voices singing back to her. Toki smiled.

"I can see her," I whispered.

"Tell me," Toki said.

I described the hill, with the trees lapping around it like waves around a rock, and the white moon shining off the snow, and the gray wolf sitting on her haunches, tail wrapped around her four paws, muzzle to the moon. "She's gone," I finished. "I hardly saw her move. Like smoke. Down the hill and in under the pine trees."

Toki thanked me, and I touched his hand because he could not see my smile. Then I turned away, wrapped myself in the cloak he'd lent me, and fell back into sleep beside the fire. Kon nuzzled me and I huddled against his hairy back, glad of his warmth. I slept and did not dream, or if I did, I forget what it was I dreamed of.

It was morning when I woke. The fires were low. Toki was cooking bread. When we had eaten it I kicked the fires apart, threw out what was left of Kon's bone, and swept up Kund's manure. While I worked, I asked Toki where he came from.

"Farther around the coast. Inland from Vegasund. My grandmother raised me. I did not know my father. My mother was a slave."

I had not seen slaves before I came to Sessing, except for once when I was little and traders passed our farm, traveling from far inland with prisoners to sell in the south. I had not liked them then, stinking and starving in their filthy rags, and what I'd seen at Sessing did not alter my opinion. They seemed to me less than human, with their empty faces and their dangling hands. And less than dogs and horses, too, of which you can grow fond, and with whom you can have some understanding, but above all, who are themselves. Slaves were none of those things. They were cowardly and stupid and fought for scraps off the floor that dogs would sniff at and pass by.

I looked at Toki, who, as I have said, was bright and beautiful. I knew that not all slaves were like the ones I'd seen. A good slave, after all, could buy his freedom in a year or two and be a free man, though many die before they can do it. But I did not want to think of Toki as the son of any slave.

"Was your grandmother a free woman?" I asked.

He shook his head. "A slave also. But one set free in her old age by a generous master. Or so they told her at the time. It meant they didn't have to feed her. It's time we went from here. Can you lead us to Smolsund? To your old home?"

Why did he call it my old home? Smolsund was still my home.

It had begun to snow outside the cave. I wished that we could stay inside, light another fire, and sleep. Too many things had happened to me one after another, and most of them were bad. I wanted to be still and warm and quiet. But I led Kund out of the cave and stood waiting, with Toki's cloak—which was ragged, being his second-best, and much too long for me—pulled up over my head and wound around my shoulders. Even so it draggled in the snow. It would soon be wet and heavy. I bent my head to keep the snow out of my eyes and stood, hunched over, moving my feet a little, hearing the snow squeak under them. A stranger looking at me, I thought, might take me for a slave.

"You ride," Toki said. "I'll walk. Kund will think himself lucky to carry you instead of me."

I looked back at the cave just once, but found no trace of my mother left in that place, and hardly any of the child I'd been when first I came there.

We passed below the hill where I had seen the wolf last night. The snow had cleared and the hill gleamed yellow in a shaft of sunlight.

"How long will it take us to reach Smolsund?" Toki asked.

"Until some time tomorrow."

"Good. We'll stop there for you to run in and show your Amma that you're safe."

"Run in? Then what? It's my home."

Toki put his hand up to Kund's neck, and stroked. "You have no home now, Ran, nor shall you for a long time. Will you curse me, I wonder, for saving you from Odin?"

"No, I never will. But why did you, Toki?"

"It seemed a pity to give you to Odin. I knew already that your hair is dark, not golden. And your eyes are light. Your nose is crooked, like my own. Your cousin Ristil, who is my good friend, or was, told me that. She warned me that you probably have a temper like your namesake. But I do not like Brokk and his choosing. I do not like his medicine and his spear and his rope. I have seen it all too many times to find it a mystery. It is murder. Besides, hooked noses have their charm."

"I don't know where to go," I said, "if I can't stay at Smolsund."

"You belong to Odin now, Ran. Anybody, hearing that, could send you to him. There may be no one left at Sessing now who knows, but we can't be sure. I go to Iceland, in the spring. There is a man there, Agnar Thorfast, he has a fine hall and I think will welcome me. I played once in his brother's hall, here in Norway. Agnar was visiting, and he liked my music. Come with me."

We walked in silence for a while. The light was waning, and I wasn't sure that I could find the valley where we'd sheltered on the way to Sessing, but the pile of rocks stood out quite clear against the snow, the bent and twisted trees crouched at its base like witches 'round a pot.

We had no fire on which to cook our meat, so our supper was the same as Kund's—raw oats. We scraped the snow out of an indentation in the rock. There was a bulge of rock above it that would give a little shelter. Kon flopped down beside us, and we wrapped ourselves and him in cloaks and blankets. We drank from Toki's flask, and talked.

"You have not yet said if you'll come to Iceland," Toki said.

"I cannot believe that I must leave my grandmother."

"We'll talk of something else. Do you know runes?"

"I know that they are marks cut on wood or stone."

"Each mark tells a story, or part of one. The runes Allfather brought back from the dead were spells as well. One to calm a stormy sea. One to put out fires. One to break chains. One to make a woman think of you, and one to keep her in your bed."

Toki took out his knife and scratched on the rock beside us.

ᚠᚢᚦᚨᚱᚲ

"This is the first, and it makes F. This one makes U, this TH, this A, this R, this K. That's why we call them the futhark. I'll teach you to cut runes and read them if you come to Iceland."

I slept then, and woke much later, very cold. I burrowed against Toki, thinking to warm myself from him while he slept. But he was not asleep. He hauled Kon in between us so that he would warm us both. Then he put his arms around me, and his face close to mine, and presently we shared our first kiss. It was the first I'd shared with anyone, apart from kissing Amma's soft cheek, or my mother.

"The morning's not far off," Toki said when we'd finished kissing. "We'll be up and off soon."

"Good," I replied. But to tell the truth, I was in no hurry for the morning.

SEVENTEEN

W E REACHED SMOLSUND early in the evening. Od was crossing the yard with a bucket of pig swill in his hand. I had forgotten how old he was and how gnarled. And how much I loved him. He looked like a twist of driftwood, leaning over his favorite sow, scratching her back with a stick. There were no strange horses in the barn, so I walked around to the back of the house and looked in at the door.

Amma was sitting by the fire, grinding barley in a hand quern. She must have sensed me standing there. She looked up, but could not see who I was. I had the light behind me.

"Ran?" she asked. "Is that you?"

"Yes, Amma."

We embraced. Inside her woollen robe Amma was light and brittle. But beautiful still, with her sharp nose and her wise eyes and her hair as soft as swans' wings. I lowered her back into her chair and knelt beside her on the floor with my arms around her middle and my cheek against her chest.

I did not know how to tell her. She is not someone from whom you hide things, to protect them. So I told her quickly. She made me tell her again and then again about the journey and the wolves, about Sessing and Gullveig and the funeral. It was as though she knew already but needed to hear it all over and over from my lips before she could bear to believe it. She put her hands over her eyes. Her knuckles were swollen from the winter's cold and from long years of work about the farm. She listened with tears running down her face, catching in the deep folds at the corners of her mouth and dripping off her chin. It was not the loss of my mother that hurt her so. It was the thought of losing me.

At last we were both quiet. I made her an infusion of sweet woodruff, which helps to soothe grief and shock. She sat sipping it and rocking. When she had finished the medicine she wiped her eyes.

"There will be time enough later for my grief," she said. "You are not safe while you stay with me. Bring your musician in."

She was on her feet again when I returned with Toki. "Welcome," she said. "Sit here and dry your clothes. Supper will soon be cooked." She watched me guide him to the chair.

Amma would not ever, even now, behave less than hospitably to any guest. Fugle's manners were not so perfect. He spat at Kon and jumped onto a roof beam.

It was a good evening. I don't know that Toki ever had so attentive an audience as Amma, Od, and me, beside the fire at Smolsund. He sang until his voice was tired, and after that he played, and the notes of his harp flew past Fugle, still perched angrily on high, and out at the smoke hole, away past the stars.

We ate and drank and pretended to be safe, which no one is, of course. We let the warmth of the fire and the shelter of the old house and the love of Amma draw the long aching of the road to come out of our bones.

EIGHTEEN

AMMA ROSE LONG before dawn, as she always did, and began to pack for us. She gave me my mother's second-best cloak and boots—her best she'd worn to Sessing. She gave us warm blankets, mead, beer, dried meat and fish, oats, barley, dried beans, and two cheeses. She gave me the spear that had been her own when she was young. I have it still. She gave us a knife, some fishing line, and her only treasure, an amber necklace. I used to want to suck the beads when I was little. They were so round and fat and yellow, like beeswax or honey.

"Amma," I said. "Not your amber necklace. You always said you would be buried with it."

"Take it," she said. "You'll need it. Amber is good to trade with everywhere." She asked Toki how we were going to find our way to Vegasund, to the ships.

"Kon carries a map of Norway in his nose," Toki said. "He knows the way to Vegasund."

"Even if that were true," said Amma doubtfully, "how will you tell him where you want to go? You're no magician, with that hooked nose of yours." Amma always said that the flat-nosed people of the north made the best magicians. She looked from Toki to me and smiled. "Though you seem to have cast a spell over my granddaughter," she added.

"If I have done that," Toki said, "I am glad. A man ought to have some reward for risking Odin's anger."

"Do not speak of it," Amma told him. "It's a bad omen. But since there is no time for courtship, I will tell you now that if my granddaughter wants you, you have my blessing. Do you, sprigget?"

"I do."

"I shall sacrifice for both of you when you are gone. Now, tell me how you're going to find your way to Vegasund."

"I'll show you," Toki told her. He took from the bottom of his sack many small parcels of cloth and hide. Each had a chip of wood sewn onto it, and each chip was cut with runes. Toki read each one with his fingertips until he found the one he wanted. He opened that parcel and unwrapped the layers of cloth until what looked like a piece of chewed boot appeared. He held it out to Kon, who sniffed it thoughtfully, licked it, nosed it again, and barked. Toki thanked him, rewrapped the scrap of leather, and put it back into his sack.

"That's it," he told us. "That's my magic."

Od understood at once because he knew dogs. "That's a good hound," he said. "Did you teach him that?"

"I did," Toki replied. "I find something for him to learn the smell of in each new place I want him to remember. He'll always lead me back."

"How did you think of it?" Od asked.

"It's a trick blind men tell each other."

"What will you do when he grows old?" Od asked.

"I'll train one of his puppies—if he sires any. His mother led me before him. And before her, his grandfather."

When everything was ready—Kon waiting in the yard, Kund loaded up—I kissed Od on the cheek, which surprised him.

I turned to Amma. Toki embraced her first. Then she and I looked at one another for a long time. We knew that it would be our last sight of each other. Amma was everything good in my childhood. What love and praise I had when I was little came from her. If I am brave, it is because she was. If I can sing a child to sleep, it is because she first sang to me. And now she made it possible for me to leave her.

"Goodbye, sprigget," she said. "I shall pray to Freya, who looks after women, every night. I shall ask her to make you a good wife to Toki, since I see you love him. I shall ask her to send you children as dear to you as you have been to me."

She watched while Toki helped me up onto Kund's back, then turned and went into the house.

Amma was my mother and my father. Amma was everything loving in my life at Smolsund. I bless her memory. I have raised a stone to her but it lies far from Smolsund, which was her home and mine.

NINETEEN

T HAT WAS A HARD PARTING. Worse have
followed it.

It took us nine days traveling to reach Toki's home. It was
a turf hut built out from the rocks, the front part roofed
with green, growing turf, the earth floor overlaid with
wood, and a lean-to stable to one side. Rowan trees grew
around the door. Bracken, dead now and rust red, hid the
step, and brambles, their leaves turned purple by the winter,
grew up and over the earthen walls and hung tangling
around the rocks, disguising the opening in the hillside.

Firewood was stacked at the back of the chamber, along-
side jars of oil and mead and barley. Smoked trout hung
from the ceiling. After we had stabled Kund, and lit a fire
and eaten, Toki fetched water from the stream. He heated it
in his beer cauldron and filled the biggest basin he pos-
sessed for me to wash in. When he asked me if I wanted
him to wait outside, it seemed ungrateful to say yes.
Besides, I thought, he can't see me.

It was wonderful to take off my stinking, itching clothes. I stood up in the basin, scooping up the hot, soft water in a bowl, pouring it over my shoulders and down my back, splashing my face, washing away the grime. When I was clean, Toki gave me a soft wrap to put around me and I sat beside the fire. If I had been Fugle I'd have purred.

"I'll heat water for you now," I said presently. I said I'd see to Kund while he washed but he said I needn't, so I stayed and watched him. He was the first man that I saw without his clothes on, and I was glad to look and not be looked at. When he asked me to wash his back I did it, and found his skin as smooth and pleasant to my hand as it had been to my eye.

"Let me wash you," he said, when I had finished.

"But I've already washed," I said.

"Let me do it again."

He washed my face first, carefully, reading it with his fingertips as if it were one of his runes. He traced my eyes, touching my lids, smoothing my eyebrows, moving his fingers up across my forehead and into my hair. I never felt so looked at as when first he touched my face. He felt my ears and stroked my cheeks and the curve of my nose and laughed, and touched my lips to see if I was smiling. He touched my chin and said he'd known by my temper that it would be strong and jutting. He washed my breasts, my hands, my feet, all of me. Then we lay down together on his bed.

Kund hung his white head over from the stable into our room and watched us. Kon had more delicacy. He stood up, threw a reproachful look at Toki, which was wasted, and went out.

I fell asleep before I knew exactly what it was that we were doing, but Toki woke me up again. He said that every new thing required practice, even this, and that we ought not to waste time. He made me laugh. He never hurried me and I felt safe with him. He said his blindness had taught him patience, but I said no, he would have been a patient man without that.

We got up at midday to feed Kon and Kund. We ate with them and sat in the pale winter sun awhile, then went back to bed. The strangeness of everything, the pleasure and the warmth of it, astonished me. It mingled with my grief at leaving Amma and I cried. Toki thought he'd hurt me, or that I was crying because of what we'd done, but I told him no, I was glad, and I asked him if he was glad too, and he said he was, very, and we had to start all over again to show each other how glad we were.

By then we were hungry again so we got up and cooked, and toasted one another with barley beer. All night the stream sang on the hill, the wind shook the rowans at the door, and the wood on the fire shifted and rustled as it burned. The whole hillside seemed to rest when we rested. A fox might bark, or an owl send its hunting call wavering out across the valley, but we lay still and safe, wrapped around each other. When I woke and looked at Toki's face, I found him smiling, and if he touched my lips with his fingers in the night, I know he found me smiling too.

It was while we lived together in his house that winter

that I began to hate his blindness. Some days it was intolerable to me that he could not see the hill behind the house, or the valley below it, or the red sky in the west at evening, or the white moon by night. And make no mistake, he knew as well as I did that he had been robbed. But that was not intolerable, he said. Intolerable means that you can't bear it. And I do bear it, he said. And so will you.

Spring came too early for us that year, but by the time it did, I knew that Amma's prayer was answered. There would be three of us, not two, taking ship for Iceland.

TWENTY

WE CAME TO VEGASUND just as the rivers were starting to melt. It terrified me when we rode in through the doorway under the great earthen rampart. I had pulled the hood of my cloak around my face, and hidden Toki's hair as best I could under his hat, but his blindness would have made him memorable if his beauty had not. If anyone in the town had heard even a whisper of Odin's chosen sacrifice, who ran off from Sessing with the blind harp player, they would know us.

We cut five beads from Amma's necklace, sold them in the market, and bought passage on the first merchant ship to leave the town. Kund kicked and fought and bit the sailors; we had a dreadful job to get him up the gangplank. There were three horses in all, and the sailors tied them head to tail down in the hold between the two half-decks. There were goats too, and sheep, and a cow. They were all fenced in forward of the mast, with food and trade goods piled behind them, and a coop of chickens. We were the only passengers.

I knew nothing of ships and Toki couldn't see to tell if ours looked sound. It was clinker-built, which means that it was made of overlapping planks fixed to ribs and cross-beams. The joints were stuffed with rope which was supposed to swell with the wet and keep the sea out. There were oars as well as a sail, and we carried water in jars and barrels, as well as food, for the journey. How long that would be depended on the wind and pirates. Four days perhaps.

Toki had to carry Kon onboard. I think that dog had sailed before. If I had known then what I know now about ships and the sea, he'd have had to carry me as well.

The sailors rowed us down the inlet and out into the fiord. Then the east wind took us and shook us and sent us slapping and splashing on our way, west and north, away from one land and toward another.

I had not known before how full of light and power the sea can be, like a watery sky lying all about you, and you a little gull dipping and wheeling, driven by the wind, which is the engine of the world.

There was no modesty aboard that ship. The sailors thought they could have fun with me, Toki being blind, and I was glad of Amma's knife. I stuck one fellow in the back of the hand and cut another on the cheek. After that they left me alone. I could have hurt them both much more if I had wanted to, but our lives were in their hands.

In the evening, when all land was beyond our sight, the wind got up. The sun slid down toward the water, with

Skoll the wolf biting his heels, the sky bled red in the west, and the seas began to rise. It was like watching hills grow. I had started being sick that morning when we were still in the fiord, and by midday I would not have minded dying. If it had not been for the baby I would have begged the great clean sea take me, prayed to my namesake to send up her net and pull us down and take us anywhere so long as it was off that heaving, lurching ship.

Late in the afternoon, sharp cramps doubled me over. I held on to Toki while the sailors fought the sea and the sea fought the ship. Great cliffs of water smashed down upon each other and the wind screamed in our rigging. I could not make Toki hear, not even by shouting in his ear, to tell him that the blood was coming. He could not see the red stain on my dress and, though I moved his hand there, we were both drenched with salt seawater so the wetness told him nothing. I hunched down on the deck with my knees up under my chin and my cloak pulled around me and howled with the storm.

They said afterward it was not a storm. More of a squall, they called it, just a wrinkle between the going of the day and the coming of the night. All sailors talk like that. But squall or storm, it took our first child. When the wind dropped, I whispered it to Toki. He held me and kissed my face and rubbed my aching back. When the morning came, he rigged my cloak up as a sort of screen and helped me wash away the blood in cold seawater.

Toki won the respect of the sailors in his own way, and for good, when he took out his harp that first morning to comfort me with music. We were bitterly cold, I more than any from seasickness and from the loss of so much blood. I hunched down inside my cloak and wished that I could die. Toki put his arms around me and rested his square chin on my head, and promised me a baby every year in Iceland, which made me cry harder because I had already loved the one I carried. So he pushed me gently aside and played his harp.

You could hardly hear the notes above the roaring of the wind, but the sailors felt it was a lucky omen to have a blind musician on the ship, and from then on I was safe with them. We ate cheese and stale bread and a vile broth of boiled salt meat, and when the chickens died on the third day, we ate them too. We drank stale water, and shoveled our ordure over the side along with that of the beasts. Each night we prayed to Ran for a steady wind and a safe landfall.

We escaped our torment briefly for one night, among the Sheep Islands. Beautiful they were, rising from the sea in sweet, soft folds of rock and earth, and I begged Toki to let us stay there. I tried to make him promise I need never set my foot on the swan's road anymore, but he said we had taken ship for Iceland and to Iceland we must go. We would have a better future there, he said. There was no land left anymore on the Sheep Islands. I was too tired and miserable to fight him.

Not long after that we saw monsters close beside us, smooth-sided beasts that shone like polished metal. They blew out jets of cloud that stood taller than trees up above their backs. They seemed like ocean gods to me. I saw the knowing eye of one of them fixed upon us as though he were wondering whether to let us cross his land or not. I called out a greeting to him, but the sailors laughed and said they'd seen men kill and eat such mountains of the sea.

We came up to the coast of Iceland in the dark. The sun rose behind us, where home lay invisible, and showed us a new land hanging low and golden, behind the gray fields of the sea.

Kund must have tasted the sweet soft grass and the brown earth on the air because he put up his head and shouted to whatever horses waited on the shore. Kon stared out angrily at what he seemed to think were water dogs, and growled. The seals looked back at him in silence. Toki and I put our arms around each other. I shut my eyes and shared with him the welcome smell of land.

Over there it was the end of what Icelanders call Cuckoo Month, the first month of the summer, when they sow their oats and barley. A new land and a new life lay before me, and I would spend it with Toki. Here I would be safe from Brokk, with his rope and his spear and his drum, and safe from Vigut with his face of the Fenris wolf.

Our ship was bound for Reykjavík, on the southwestern seaboard of Iceland in the great bay of Faxaflói. All that day we sailed with land close to the north and then the west of us, while the livestock, and particularly Kund, grew more restless and impatient. Then the wind dropped and it looked as though we'd suffer one more hateful night onboard, but the sailors pulled out oars and rowed us into harbor.

We were strangers in a strange land. It is a lonely feeling. But it was good to have earth under my feet, although it still seemed to heave and toss like water. Kund clattered down the gangplank with his ears back and the whites of his eyes showing. His gray coat was crusted with salt and he'd lost what little fat he'd carried when he came onboard. Kon stayed close to Toki, nuzzling his hand from time to time, begging, I dare say, never to go to sea again.

We traveled over land up the west coast of Iceland, heading always north toward Hvam, a journey of ten days. We stopped at farms and settlements when we came across them, and Toki's music earned us a warm welcome beside every fire. The custom of the people here is much the same as back in Norway when it comes to strangers. They must be fed and sheltered, however poor the host may be.

Always we asked directions for Thorsdale, Agnar Thorfast's hall. As we drew nearer to it, we heard he was a good man and well liked by all his neighbors. His hall stood in the shelter of Helga Fell, the holy mountain, looking out across a narrow fiord. He had a sheltered harbor there from which to launch his trading ship, and good farming land with pasture in the hills behind.

It was a fine place, not so grand as Sessing, nor so old, but far bigger than Smolsund. Both of us felt afraid when we reached it, though neither of us said so. On his own, Toki would have been sure of a warm welcome. But traveling musicians do not usually bring their wives with them. We could only hope that I might earn my share of hospitality in the kitchen while Toki earned his in the hall.

We walked together up the hill with Kon and Kund beside us. The hall was built of turfs resting on low stone walls. The beam ends I could see under the turf roof were unlike any wood that I had ever seen. Later, I learned that they were bones of sea creatures bigger even than those we had seen from the ship. The turf roof made a long green hillside; smoke rose up as though from underground. Three great columns of bone leaned by the door—they were sea beasts' tusks, from the narwhal, but I took them for the teeth of some land monster and wondered what kind of country I had come to.

A woman was scraping sealskins on a wooden frame out in the yard. Behind her a boy trimmed firewood with an axe and threw it up onto a high pile. They stopped work when they heard Kon's hooves on the track and watched us approach.

I had already told Toki what the place looked like. Now I told him of the woman and the boy, and asked if I should speak to them.

"No. Stand behind me like a proper wife and let me speak," he said. So I did.

We knew we must look a poor sight, dirty and sickly from traveling, with a thin dog and a bony wreck of a horse at our heels. But Toki took his harp out of its leather sack and held it in his hand to show the people his trade, and the boy smiled and ran indoors. When he came back out, a big man, tall and heavy with a long fair beard, was with him. I guessed by his fine red cloak, dyed with the madder that grows in Iceland, and by his silver arm band that he must be Agnar Thorfast.

TWENTY-ONE

WE STAYED AT THORSDALE all through Cuckoo Month, and up until the end of egg-time. It was a good place. Agnar Thorfast had brought finely carved roof posts with him from Norway, which made the hall feel as though it had stood there for longer than it had. Between the two rows of carved posts a fire always burned, and the thick wood smoke billowed up into the roof and crept out through the smoke hole—or else it billowed around the hall, making all the people cough and wipe their eyes. It depended on which way the wind was blowing.

The walls were built of turf blocks set on a low stone foundation, and there were window holes which could be shut with wooden shutters on cold days. The floor was earth, with wooden planks laid over it. Benches were built into the long walls for the men, with cross-benches on the short walls for the women. Everyone ate and slept together in the main hall. Only Agnar and Asa, his wife, had curtains around their bed. Weaving was done at one end of the hall, not in a separate weaving room. Asa had plans to make Agnar build on more rooms—a better privy, a dairy, and more pens for the beasts. There was already a good barn, where the slaves slept with the cattle, as well as a smithy.

Toki played and sang each evening in the hall for Agnar and his guests. And always at his elbow hovered Gulli, the boy who'd run in smiling when we came, watching and learning, drinking in Toki's music like water from a spring. Of course he had no harp of his own, but he had pipes that he'd made himself, and a strong voice, and he begged lessons from Toki whenever the two of them were free. Toki taught him gladly. He told Gulli that he'd make a good enough musician if he'd only practice more. But he told me Gulli was the best pupil he had ever taught.

I worked hard in the kitchen, cooking, making cheeses, drying herbs, curing meat, washing clothes, sweeping floors. Outdoors I planted, hoed, weeded, and watered. When no other work was given me to do I spun and wove. Toki's work was to please his master's ear. Mine was to please his belly, and I know which of us had the better bargain. But it was a good household, run with justice and good humor.

Agnar and Asa had both sons and daughters, but all were away from home except for the two youngest, Mord and Sif. Mord was a fair-haired lad of fourteen, a good boy but always running after girls. Sif, his sister, was twelve years old, quiet and serious, with her father's gray eyes. She was already more a woman than a child, and had a way of looking at you when you spoke to her that let you know she heard more than you said. I liked her straightaway.

There was also Asa's widowed sister with her children, and a foster son of Agnar's, as well as two of his nephews. There were a dozen or so paid laborers and a shifting population of slaves. Agnar was a fair master and would let any good worker earn his freedom, or buy it if he had the money. Several of the slaves had borne children, but Asa would not put them out to die, even though Agnar said Thorsdale was not large enough for everyone who lived there. "Leave them alone," Asa would say. "We can sell them when they're grown."

"And until then I must feed them, and they do next to nothing for their keep," Agnar would grumble. But he did not insist.

Ruling over all of them was Asa's mother, an ancient wisp of a woman with black eyes and white hair who spent her time propped in a chair beside the fire. She was the oldest person I had seen, and I was frightened of her.

Agnar's father had been a friend of the first big settler into Iceland, whose name was still the best-known in the land. This man had given Agnar's father a good piece of land, and Agnar made it prosper. Now the family owned land both in the hills and on the coast, as well as a trading ship that carried timber and soapstone out from Norway and took back woollen cloth, seal oil, ivory, and falcons. The falcons of Iceland are everywhere known to be the best.

Agnar's men would bring captured falcons in boxes and cages for sale across the sea. They were solitary creatures of the wide sky, shut into foul-smelling darkness, their great eyes mad with longing for the clouds and the rain, hungry for the rush of air and the sea crawling below, and the soar and dive of the hunt. My favorites were the great white gyrfalcons. "Only bear the voyage," I would tell them, "and you'll be free at least to hunt, though you never see home again."

Falcons are brave birds. Many of them would neither eat nor drink in captivity and died long before they reached the markets of the mainland. No doubt that is why they are so valuable.

I was a servant in the house, but I learned much by listening to what was said around me about the land we'd come to. Toki learned more in the hall each evening, among the guests and travelers who passed through Agnar's ever-open door to sit at Asa's generous table. Thorsdale was always crowded. Time alone with Toki was more precious than amber. I tried not to think of home and Amma until I was alone, or safe with Toki in our bed in the barn by night.

When Cuckoo Month was over and the oats and barley sown, I went with the other women several times to gather seabirds' eggs. At home in Norway, egg-time had been the work of men, because of the steep cliff climbing. Here the birds were so plentiful that it was more like picking fruit. We tied big baskets on our backs and walked among the rocks where the birds nested, taking eggs from every nest but never leaving any empty.

It was a chance to talk and rest a little, away from Asa's eyes. A time for making friends and telling stories. I worked with Sigrid who, like me, had been born in Norway. She had come to Iceland when she was fifteen to marry a man called Ulf. Her brother had chosen him for her and she did not like him much, but made the best of it. Her only real sorrow was to have no children after three long years of marriage.

On our third day out, Sigrid led me to a tumbled ruin. I did not like the look of it, but she took my hand and asked me to go with her. She took nine eggs from her basket and put them carefully down in what must have been the doorway of the hut. She whispered something under her breath and turned away.

"What was that for?" I asked her.

"A woman died in childbirth here. The place is haunted. No one will live here anymore so the hut has fallen down. But if you make an offering here—eggs, a carved doll, a piece of cloth—the woman's spirit will sometimes help you bear a child."

"Then I pray she will help you, Sigrid."

"The child she died of was her ninth. Nine is a powerful number. If nine eggs don't work, I'll bring her a length of good cloth."

A few months later, when she knew neither the eggs nor the cloth had worked, Sigrid began to sleep with other men than Ulf, in the hope that this might bring success. It was a risky business, and he would probably have sold her into slavery if he had caught her. But she felt that it was worth the risk. One of the men taught her to cut runes and they used to leave each other messages, arranging where to meet and when. I reminded Toki then that he had promised to teach me, and we began our lessons. It isn't hard to learn; you only need someone to show you the shapes.

Sigrid told me about Iceland, of which she'd heard much

but seen little. At first I thought she was a liar, but afterward I found that all of what she said was true. Inland, she told me, is mostly mountains, and you cannot live there. There are hardly any animals on the land, apart from those the settlers brought, but the coast and all the lakes and rivers teem with fish and wild birds. There are seals for the taking, and great whales beach themselves around the coast.

There are places where hot water bubbles up out of the ground—this I did not believe until I saw it with my own eyes. And there are other places, spirit-haunted, which make a sound like rushing wind and spit water high into the air. There are mud holes and steam holes which lead down to a boiling pit of fire. Sometimes, Sigrid told me, whole mountains open up, spewing red rock and melted stone from that dreadful region out into the air.

Toki often sang and played till morning, with Gulli always close beside him. It does not get dark during egg-time in Iceland, and Agnar Thorfast's guests would keep him late and early. I would stand at the back of the hall with a distaff held in the crook of my left arm, twirling my spindle with its stone disc and winding the thread up into a big ball every time the spindle reached the floor. I had none of Sigrid's worries. I knew already that another child was on its way.

TWENTY-TWO

AGNAR WAS AWAY ALL shieling-time, fetching timber from Norway, so it was Asa who decided that Toki and I should take the sheep up to the hills to graze. Agnar would be back in time for haymaking and corn cutting. If he missed his music too much, he could send for Toki. I could stay up with the sheep till Autumn Month.

It was what we'd hoped for. Sheep are easy work, though it would all be mine. Asa lent us a loom and gave us flour and fish hooks, three hens and a cockerel in a wicker cage, two kids, and as much firewood as Kund could carry. I felt at last that our long journey was over. Ahead lay safety, and a new life.

"You've worked hard here," Asa told me. "If you can make a go of it with a blind husband, I'll give you the shieling. It's a good place. It's called Frey's Field."

We liked each other, Asa and I, despite the difference in our ranks. Besides, she needed someone she could trust out on the fringes of her land. "You can grow a little food, and catch what you can't grow. The river there is full of fish."

"Now we have everything we need," I said to Toki as we packed. "We have each other. We have land of our own. And we have a child coming." He had not known of it till then. He put down the loom and embraced me.

We loaded Asa's gifts onto Kund's back, and set off early in the morning. Kon was not so fine a sheepdog as he was a hunter, but he did his best, and Asa let Gulli go with us to show us the way. Kon and Gulli ran on ahead, keeping the sheep and the kids in a tightly moving bunch. When I could see that they were managing, and would lose none of the flock, I climbed onto Kund's back and rode. My feet had swelled a little and I felt the heat. Toki twined his brown hand into Kund's white mane and strode along beside us, singing quietly.

The shieling, when we reached it in the evening, was a one-room stone hut standing on the side of a hill with its back to a great wall of rock that pierced the short grass. The hill behind looked kind and sheltering, and above it stretched the blue Icelandic sky. At the front the hillside dropped down, steep and rocky, to the river, where the valley opened out like rich green cloth. Buttercups shone around the doorstep.

There was a stone pen built on at one end of the hut which would make a stable if we repaired the roof where winter storms had broken down the turfs. On either side of the house there was a little flat land, just enough for growing oats or hay. Wood for the fire would be a problem. There were few trees inland, and no peat to cut. We'd have to find a way to buy it or earn it, and bring it up from the

coast. Water must be close by, because although I couldn't
see it, I could hear a stream. All summer lay before us.
Winter would bring the child. We were happy.

We unloaded Kund and made him comfortable, and then
sat down outside the house on the short turf, watching the
sheep spread out on the hillside. We ate the bread and
dried fish we'd brought with us, and drank the beer Sigrid
had hidden in our pack. I set some of each aside to offer the
guardian spirits of the place before Toki and I should cross
the threshold of our home.

Gulli was in no hurry to go back to Thorsdale. He would
have stayed with Toki until Autumn Month if we'd let him,
talking music and playing Toki's harp. But I did not want
him to walk home in the dark. And besides, he would be
wanted back at Thorsdale. We made him go when he had
finished eating.

"He's a good boy," Toki said, when the sound of the lad's
footsteps had faded away. I did not answer, and he sent his
hand down to nestle warmly in my dress. I leaned down to
kiss him and we said no more. It was a great luxury for us to
be alone together. The sun warmed our faces and the grass
under my back was soft and cool and sweet.

When the sun lost its warmth and the light grew dim, we
poured beer and crumbled bread to the north, south, east,
and west of our new home, in greeting to the spirits of the
place, and went indoors.

Standing in our doorway while Toki lit the fire, I told
him all that I could see. The valley lay as green as moss
under the red light of sunset, and the river shone like
bronze. The hills grew softer, rounder, lower, in the west

toward the coast, where lay Thorsdale and the sea, hidden by distance and an evening mist as dim and blue as faded cloth. A fiord glinted like a needle piercing the hem of the land. Out there, I told him, in the west, great whales graze the endless ocean like cattle of the gods. To the east, across the land, over the sea, lies Norway, and Smolsund. And Amma sits there by her fire, seeing the same red sun go down over the same cold sea. But I shall not see her again this side of death.

We fed the hens and shut them in the house with us. Kon eyed them but knew better than to chase them. He had dried fish again that night, and bread, the same as us, while Kund ate sweet grass out on the hillside.

We made ourselves a bed beside the fire, of cloaks and blankets piled on some clean straw we found in the pen. I lay beside Toki and held his strong brown hand and felt his fingertips that drew such beauty from his harp.

"You're sad, Ran," he said presently. "Don't be sad. You are my good wife, even if we have not married. And your grandmother will soon be a great-grandmother. All her prayers are answered."

We slept then, lying close beside each other. As I closed my eyes, I prayed that I might sleep all the nights of my life next to Toki. But I dreamed about the wolf from Iron Wood and woke sweating with fear.

I got up quietly, so as not to wake Toki, took my spear, and walked out to stand under the porch. Kon padded at my heels. The meadow looked cool and silver in the moonlight and as I stepped out to breathe the night scent of the grass, something brushed against my cheek. I jerked away, thinking perhaps it was a snake—though there are none in Iceland—or a spider's web. I cannot bear the touch of spiders; it makes no difference to me that they will not hurt me. The thing had caught in my hair, and as I pulled away, it slithered down and fell into the grass. It was only an old leather belt which someone had forgotten and left hanging from the porch beam. As I bent to pick it up, the moonlight shone on the bronze strap-end, and I saw that it was stamped with the face of a wolf.

The foul, sweet smell of bear's fat filled my nose. Kon sniffed the belt and growled. He growled again, deep in his chest, his lip pulled back off his strong dog teeth.

Toki was up and standing by me in a second. The foul, sweet smell of bear's fat disappeared. The river glittered under a full moon and the sheep lay silent on the hillside. I shook, and my head pounded the way it used to when my mother beat me.

"It's all right," Toki said. "It's all right. Tell me what you dreamed off. That will make you less afraid."

"I dreamed about the Fenris wolf. I woke up and came outside to shake the dream off, and something touched my face. This leather belt. It smelled of Vigut, Toki. It smelled of bear's fat when I picked it up."

Toki ran the belt through his fingers, felt the embossed wolf's head, and touched the leather to his nose. "It's dusty, that's all. It smells of nothing but old leather, Ran."

"It's his belt, Toki. It smelled of him. He's been here to our house, Toki. He came to find us and he knows we're here."

"Plenty of men wear belts with embossed strap-ends. Plenty of strap-ends are embossed with wolves' heads."

"I smelled the bear's fat of his beard, Toki."

Toki lifted the belt to his nose and sniffed again. "It smells of dust and leather. You imagined the smell of bear's fat because of the dream."

I began to cry then, with relief, and Toki put his arms around me and took me back to bed. But still I could not sleep.

"What if he came to Iceland, Toki?" I asked presently.

"He did, Ran. He came some time ago."

All my happiness, all my saftey drained away from me. "Vigut is here? In Iceland? You heard that and you told me nothing?"

"You were happy. I did not want to frighten you. He's far up to the north. He's long ago forgotten us. We'll never see him, Ran."

"Would you let a child play beside a wolf, Toki? Just because the child was happy? We are the children, Toki. Vigut is the wolf."

"I heard he's taken land up in the north, at Stad on Skagafiord. What reason would he have to come down here?"

"What if he finds us, Toki?"

"Why should he even look?"

I dreamed no more of the Fenris wolf and tried hard to forget Vigut. I taught Toki how to card and clean wool, how to spin thread on a distaff, and how to weave. There was no one there to see. I picked madder to make red dye and lichen for violet, and I found mud in the valley that would give us black from its iron. We cut grass and made hay together to keep Kund through the winter, and I caught fish in the river. We ate it fresh, and smoked enough to take us through the cold time. I picked what berries I could find, and wild leeks, and took seed from some of the wild grasses. The goats had mated—we would have a kid soon—and the hens had raised a brood each.

Frey's Field was prospering and Toki praised me often for the way I worked. The sheep were strung out far across the hills. It would be hard to round them up and drive them back to Thorsdale, but Asa would send Gulli up to help me. She would know I would be big by then and slower on my feet.

That summer it seemed that we had everything we wanted. Our own shieling. A fire to share in the evenings. A bed to share at night. Children coming, boys and girls. A baby every year, Toki had promised me.

I will not say it was a lazy summer. In Iceland survival depends on cattle but prosperity grows on the backs of the sheep. Meat fills your belly; cloth fills your purse. We had goats, which are poor men's cattle, for meat, milk, and hides. When Toki's weaving improved we would begin to build our little share of wealth. There was no one to laugh at us because he did the woman's work, and I the man's. At night we did as we liked, joyfully, though I found I had to turn my back on him as my belly grew.

I found a little lake, a pool, a puddle really, caught in a cup of the hill behind Frey's Field, and we swam there. But best of all was the hot spring I found close by the shieling—that was the water I'd heard bubbling and running our first night. The spring came out of the ground between two rocks and ran over a little bed of gravel away down the hill. I went there to fetch water the first morning and saw steam rising from it. Sigrid had told me about water coming hot out of the ground but I had not believed her. I put my hand near the water, felt the warmth rising, and ran shouting back to Toki.

We hollowed out a bathing place in the gravel below the spring. There are few things more delightful, when your belly is large and your feet ache, than sitting in a pool of clear warm water, feeling the sun on your back. Also we dug a channel and took the water close to the house. It was cold by the time it reached our door, but clean water running past your house is a great blessing.

I had misjudged the time the child was due. It was still Corn Cutting Month, and not quite into autumn, when she came.

TWENTY-THREE

GUDRUN, WE NAMED HER, and gave three hens to Freya, the mother goddess. I was beside the spring when it began. I had woken feeling heavy, as if a sack of grain were slung between my legs, dragging me down toward the earth. I went outside to pass water, and then walked slowly up the hill.

Mist in the valley hid the river. Our hill, Frey's Field, and the rock behind, all floated. The sun would not look over the hill again until the springtime, but there was a gap between the hills to my right, to the north, and I knew that if I waited I would see a shaft of light come through and touch the mist. I stood, feeling the weight between my legs, with one hand on my belly and one in the small of my back. I had a dull ache, low in my back, but no more.

Nothing prepared me for the hot, sharp clench of pain that twisted up the middle of my body, bending me double, prickling my face with sweat, making me shake and dance like Gullveig. I couldn't make a sound until it passed. Then I cupped my hands and shouted, deep and hoarse. Toki came running, barefoot, pulling on his clothes. Before he got to me I was bent double again, teeth clenched, exploding. I must have made some sound because he came straight to me, held me, told me it was going to be all right.

"What would you know about it, you blind fool?" I choked out when the pain had passed. "You only put it there. It's me that's got to fetch it out!" All women say such things in labor.

The poor man tried to make me come indoors but I would not. I made him take my skirt and socks off and sit me in the spring. I screamed at him each time he tried to lift me out. Toward the end, when I could feel a hard, round mountain bursting me apart, I told him it was finished, I was dying, and hit him when he smiled. He pulled me out of the water, then reached down and felt between my legs while I summoned what strength I could to hit him again. Before he could tell me what he felt, the child's head burst through my noose of straining muscle, and both of us were free. Her shoulders followed, first one, then the other. Toki lifted her up and laid her on my belly. He pulled his jerkin off and laid it over her, and put his own head down beside her.

It began to rain then, gently, but we could not move. We lay, hearing the birds above us, and Gudrun's little squeaks and rustles. I was not expecting any more pain and, when it came, I thought at first it meant another child. But it was just what follows any birth. Toki bit the cord through with his teeth and helped me back into the house.

He carried Gudrun, still wrapped in the jerkin. He lit the fire, fetched the soft cloths we had prepared, and wrapped her in them, then brought water from the spring, washed me, and fed me soup. He sang while I fed Gudrun.

She knew exactly what to do; I was amazed at how powerful her suck was. I began to tell Toki what she looked like, but he did not want to learn her by words. Instead he touched her softly, laying the back of his forefinger against her cheek while she sucked and snuffled, smoothing her wisps of hair, red like his own, and damp, delicately tracing the small, closed eyes, the minute nose, until she put her hand up and caught his finger and held it with the strength new babies have, which surprises us each time we feel it.

Gulli came back just three weeks later to help me bring the sheep in off the hill. By then I could tie Gudrun to my back. Toki stayed in the house, cursing his blindness.

"It is not fair," he snarled, "that you should be the man and bear the children too."

He cheered up when Gulli told him Agnar was back and planning a feast to welcome in the winter. "You'll be the chief musician, Toki," the boy said. "I'm to bring the sheep down to Thorsdale, and you are to come with me. Everyone speaks of you. Agnar says there's nobody can touch you for singing, and they won't hear of feasting without your music. Ran is to stay at Frey's Field, Asa says, because she should not have to travel yet with the new baby."

That was kind of Asa. But I was afraid for Toki in the great hall without me. I knew that he had managed well enough before he snatched me off the gallows tree. But we had grown used to being together. Who would help him when I wasn't there? As a matter of fact, Toki had never been short of women offering their help and more. That frightened me as well. And what would it be like for me, alone with Gudrun? What if I dreamed of the Fenris wolf again? What if I smelled bear's fat in the night? What did Vigut know, up on Skagafiord? Did he know there was a blind musician with a dark-haired wife down in the south of Iceland? He could not hope to prosper if he knew and did nothing. Allfather would not let him.

Even so, Toki left Kon and Kund with me and Gudrun, and walked down with Gulli and the sheep to Thorsdale for the festival. I dreamed no dreams and smelled no smells, and spent my days at work with Gudrun on my back, and my evenings playing with her, and my nights listening to her quiet snore and snuffle before I, too, fell asleep.

By the time Toki returned I had brought the goats into the pen, killed one and smoked the meat, checked over all our winter stores of fish and wild birds, smoked and salted, dressed the goat hide ready to make winter boots, and prepared butter and skyr, the cheesy curds he liked, to take us through till spring.

It was fuel for the fire I was most wanting and he brought a long sledge piled high with it, pulled by one of Agnar's horses, as well as two more loads brought up by Thorsdale slaves. They were new faces, from Ireland, they said. Agnar had bought them in Norway. They were strong-looking men and hoped to buy their freedom with a

111

few years of labor. Their names were Flight and Fiddle—not their born names, I suppose, but that's what Agnar called them.

That winter we made skis and snowshoes, and sent Kon hunting though there was precious little game. We had not enough hay for Kund, and before spring came we had to slaughter him. We were both sad, not only because we loved the old horse, but because we needed him. I let his life out gently, with a sharp knife, while Toki held his head and stroked behind his ears and blessed and thanked him for the work he'd given us.

Gudrun watched, not understanding, from her nest in the hay. It was quickly done, and kindly. You cannot let a good horse starve. Besides, we might need his meat ourselves, if the winter was a long one. I raised a stone to him, and Toki did not laugh at me. I cut the runes myself. They said:

THIS STONE IS RAISED TO KUND
OUR GOOD GRAY HORSE.
HE CAME WITH US FROM NORWAY.
BETTER HORSE HAD NO MAN.

When Cuckoo Month came around again, Gudrun was almost walking, and the next baby was making my back ache, though it hardly showed in the curve of my belly. Gudrun was small and plump, with red hair like her father, and the beginnings of a curve to her small nose. She had my temper and her father's smile, and I saw Amma in her face. The likeness did not lie in one particular feature or another, but rather in the way she looked out at the world. There was a look of recognition in her eye when she looked up at Kon's gray muzzle or down into the spring while I was washing her, which made me think of Amma looking at her garden, or Amma in the kitchen, baking bread. She was at home in the world, as Amma had been.

In Haymaking Month Agnar sent Flight and Fiddle to us with a colt to train. Toki liked beasts. His quiet ways taught them more than any man with two good eyes and a whip could, and Agnar knew it. This colt was a beauty, sturdy and strong, with a thick, upright mane and a tail that would sweep the ground when he was just a little older. Agnar had bought him for a fighter, but he proved too good for that.

Horsefighting was a sport new to me and Toki. In Norway it would have been thought a waste to make good horses fight each other. A waste of men also, sometimes, for the handlers must fight too, each with his own horse against the other, and both man and beast are often spoiled before the fight is finished.

We put the colt in the pen and asked Flight and Fiddle in to eat with us. Agnar had told them they must stay and help us cut the grass if it was ready, though he could only spare them for a day or two. Haymaking and corn cutting are busy times, with grass to scythe and rake and turn, and then to be dragged back on carts and sledges to the barns, or built into stacks and thatched against the winter. They were glad to stay the night, and I was glad to have them at Frey's Field, for they brought me good news from Sigrid. She had her child at last, a son named Slodi.

I cooked a stew of young birds I had netted down by the river, and we drank to Sigrid's health in beer she'd sent with Flight and Fiddle. Gudrun sat next to Fiddle on her sheep-skin rug beside the fire, dipping her fingers in his beer and listening to the talk.

The news was all fighting in the north, up on Skagafiord. Raiders had been killing settlers there, taking their land. Land-hungry people don't care what the law says. Then, as though the fighting over land had not brought blood-shed enough, the mountainside had opened up and thrown down fire and rocks onto the farms below, covering the fields with a blanket of dead rock. All the crops were spoiled and men were coming south, settlers and raiders both, driving what beasts they still had with them, hungry for new land to farm.

"Does Agnar expect trouble?" Toki asked. "Does he think they'll come to Thorsdale?"

"He says we must be ready," Fiddle answered, gently lift-ing his mug out of Gudrun's reach. "He said to tell you that he'll try to send a warning if it looks like starting, so that you can come back down to Thorsdale. But I doubt there'll be much time for messages. If I were you I'd watch for smoke down on the coast, and if you see it, run."

One or two stragglers had already reached Thorsdale, Flight said. They spoke with horror of the fire that fell over their farms, burying their fields with ash, stifling their beasts, killing their crops. But more than the mountain, they feared the raiders. I picked up Gudrun, who was sleep-ing now, and sat with her warm and heavy in my arms.

Flight shook his head. "They want land," he said, "and

when they find it, they kill everyone on it. One of the women told me how it was. Her man was off on the sea and she was bringing in the hay with her children. She'd gone into her house to fetch food out for them and she happened to look up from the fire. She saw men with swords standing away on the edge of her fields. She ran to the door and shouted, but her children didn't hear her. Before she could run out, the men were in the field and her children were dead. She hid under the floor of her storehouse, waiting until dark, so as to creep out to the field in case her children still lived. Later she hoped they were all dead because the men made a fire and burned their bodies. She got away once they had found her ale. She says their leader is a dreadful man. Even his own men fear him. He's bringing all the raiders south toward the better land. Our land. They say he has a powerful magician with him, and his weapons are the best. His shield is decorated with a wolf's head, and they say that neither sword nor spear can pierce it."

TWENTY-FOUR

MORNING AND EVENING, all that winter, I climbed the hill behind Frey's Field to scan the western sky for smoke. Once the snow had fallen I took snow-shoes, and sticks to lean on. Toki came with me, carrying Gudrun on his back to keep her from the snow. He was afraid that I might fall, my labor being near.

I began to have terrible dreams of children, always of children, running, running, and my little Gudrun running with them, and men with swords behind them. In front of the men, close, close to my Gudrun's heels, there ran a wolf with strong white teeth. I would wake screaming with the stink of bear's fat in my nose.

This time I knew when the child was coming. It began at night. At first I did not even wake Toki, but lay trying not to clench myself against the pain, watching Toki, watching Gudrun. They lay side by side on the sleeping platform we had made down one side of the room, wrapped in sheep-skin rugs, their faces closed and distant as faces are in sleep.

The last of the fire flickered now and then. Kon snored, his big paws in the ashes.

This time was easier and faster. I woke Toki when my waters broke, gushing warmly out between my legs, soaking my skirt, easing the weight of pressure that I felt up where the baby lay. Toki moved himself gently off the platform without waking Gudrun. He came and sat behind me so that I could lean against him, reaching his arms around to stroke my hard belly, rocking gently with my rocking, pressing his curly beard into my neck, holding me when I grunted.

Gudrun woke toward the end although I did my best to make no noise. She sat up, watching us. Kon, who was not allowed onto the platform and had lost his place beside the fire to us, sat by the door like a faithful old slave on guard, and did not stir until the child was born.

Toki reached down and lifted it the last little way out. I lay back against him with my eyes shut, promising for the second time that this would be the last. His hands moved slowly, delicately, over the warm, wet child.

"A boy," he said, "this one's a boy."

I opened my eyes and looked down at the slippery little creature. The child opened his eyes at the same moment and we were caught in one another's gaze. Then he sneezed. Toki got up, fetched soft, warm cloths, wrapped the baby up, and gave him to me.

"Gudrun's awake," I told him, and he smiled and called her over.

"Come on," he called, "come here and see your brother."

Gudrun climbed down and staggered over to us. She sat

herself on Toki's knee and watched the baby, who was feeding now. Presently she got up and came to me. She put her hand out, touched his small, bald head, and then his hand, uncurled his fingers carefully, sniffed at the faint, salt smell of him. She pushed my shirt aside and sucked for a few moments at my other breast, then returned to her father's lap and sat, thumb in mouth, eyelids drooping. The next time I looked up she was asleep.

"Do you still want to call him Grim?" I asked. That was his choice for a boy.

Toki nodded. "Before she had me, my mother had another son. She called him Grim. He didn't live long."

"What did he die of?"

"Of not being wanted—except by his mother. He was born in winter, food was very short that year, and they put him out to die."

"No one will ever put our Grim out."

"You do not know what waits for him, Ran. Nor for Gudrun."

"No. I'm glad I don't."

When Grim was four weeks old, and looked set to stay with us, we killed a kid to welcome him. If it had been later in the year we would have eaten outside by the spring, to honor the spirit of Frey's Field, and poured mead into the water for a blessing. But the snow was still on the ground so we made up a good fire indoors and left food and wine outside on the step for whatever gods or spirits might be out and about in the frost and dark.

I think we felt as safe that night as people can. It was the last time that we did. We built the fire carelessly, knowing the cold time to be nearly over. I baked the meat and we ate all we wanted. Kon cracked bones beside us, thumping his master with his bony tail from time to time in thanks. Grim sucked and slept at my breast to his own rhythm. Gudrun sat up straight between Toki and me, chewing her morsels carefully. Young as she was, and small, she brought something of Amma, her great-grandmother, to the party.

When we had finished eating, Toki took his harp out of its leather bag and played for us. First Gudrun sang, a small song of her own making, wordless and tuneless. Then Toki sang the story of the goddess Idunn and her golden apples that keep the gods forever young. I think he wanted, for those hours beside the fire, to dream that life might stay the way it was—him and me, Gudrun and Grim. Love, food, and fire.

Two mornings after that I saw a thread of smoke down by the sea.

TWENTY-FIVE

I WANTED TO RUN SOUTH, away from the smoke. I tried to believe that we could live somehow until we found a farm to take us in. "I can work hard," I said to Toki. "You know I can. They'd only have to look at me to see that I can work."

"The cold would kill us all before we reached a farm. And if it didn't, who would take us in? Men who are fighting for their land don't want blind men and babies."

"Why not stay here and hope they pass us by?"

"Agnar Thorfast took us in and gave us land. How can we hide while he is attacked? And even if we could, our best chance lies with him at Thorsdale. All the outlying farms would fight with Agnar."

If only we had known what was to come.

"What will they do to us if we lose, Toki?"

"Why ask? You know the answer."

We left the barn door open so the goats could get out to find water, and we spread what hay we had where they could reach it. We put the chickens into baskets and tied them on the colt. We put Gudrun on his back and fastened her there with a length of cloth, along with our bedding and the harp. Toki carried Grim.

We were soon away. The sun hung close to the horizon. Yellow streaked the sky inland. Down the coast the smoke rose black and evil like a rune cut in the winter sky. I did not let myself imagine what was happening beneath it.

By the time we reached Thorsdale, a heavy snow was falling. If we had waited for a day we might not have made it down from Frey's Field. If we had waited for a day we might have been safe, and I might not be going home alone.

We asked Thor to send more and heavier snow, as thick and wild as pleased him, with hail and gale and tempest besides. Storms would protect us. As long as all the ways over the hills and up the valleys were blocked we would have time to prepare.

Agnar greeted us kindly at the door and put us to work fetching water from the spring. It wasn't far from the main hall, but if the raiders fought us to the door they could deny us water. Sigrid and I and many other women fetched water in leather buckets and filled barrels, as many as we could find to fill. Thirst kills before hunger. So does fire.

Supplies of everything were low, as they must be at the end of winter. There was very little salt fish, but there were still a few beasts Agnar had kept through the winter, and these were driven in from the home field to the yard and penned behind the house. They would feed us for a little while. Agnar did not expect the fight to last long. If they drove us back into the hall they would burn it, and us with it.

Everyone in Thorsdale, free or slave, old or young, woman or man, had work to do. Agnar wanted the wall that ringed the hall repaired and closed. We fetched stone, heaved boulders, sweated and struggled, closed the gateway, mended every weak point right around the yard, and raised the height of the wall by as much stone as we could lay our hands on. Everyone worked together. Flight, Fiddle, and the other slaves; Gulli and all the laborers; Agnar and Asa's son Mord; their daughter Sif; Ulf, and Sigrid, who like me worked with a child on her back. Toki too, fetching and carrying stone to mend and raise the wall.

At night the men mended shields and sharpened swords and spears. The women did what women do, cooking and cleaning, minding children, listening to one another's troubles. We also sharpened spears. Toki sang for us, and sometimes Sif, Agnar's solemn daughter, danced. That was the only time her grandmother smiled. I think she knew what we were facing, though her old face was unreadable and she almost never spoke.

There was little fuel left, so our fires were small and the nights were cold. The slaves slept in the hall with the rest of us. I kept Gudrun wrapped up so that she could hardly move, and Grim was always tied to my back or his father's, underneath our shirts. When I could shake off my fear for a moment I was glad to be with Sigrid and the others. I had missed the company of women. Sigrid's baby son, Slodi, was as sweet as any child. Sigrid thought him extraordinary and the time came, and soon, when I had heard enough, and more than enough, about his teeth and bowels. Still, I tried to listen patiently. She had waited four slow years for him.

It was nine days before the raiders came. We killed the three best horses and offered them to Thor. We asked him for more snow, and for the first time that I could remember he answered our prayers. The sky thickened to something like a ploughed field, yellow snow clouds blotted out the mountains and the sea, snow drove in under eaves, around shutters, hissing through the roof hole and down into the fire. Agnar's old mother sat in her chair watching the fizz and spit, her black eyes looking somewhere else—into the past maybe. Or, maybe, the future.

On the eighth day the wind blew harder than I'd ever known it. The willow bushes all around the yard bent level with the snow, turves flew off the roof, and one of the barns fell, crushing the animals inside it. The wind scraped us like a knife, cutting the snow clouds from the sky, scouring the high dome clean, building the snow into waves, sharp, white, and higher than the hall.

Then the wind died and a pale Icelandic sun crept part way up the sky, telling us winter had turned, and spring was on the way. The shine on the snow forced us to close our eyes to narrow slits. The mountains behind us seemed suddenly near, as they do in clear weather, and the sea came close enough to taste. Sound carried endlessly. On the morning of the ninth day we heard a wolf calling, a lonely, desperate voice crying out for comfort.

I was standing on the long table, mending the roof with scraps of timber Fiddle passed to me. Gudrun sat under the table on Kon's back. At the cry of the wolf the old dog leaped up, growling, and threw Gudrun off.

"Wolf won't hurt you," I murmured, kissing her forehead. She had bumped it hard. "He's away out in the snow, looking for his friends, that's all. Isn't he, Fiddle?"

Fiddle made a sign I didn't recognize, some childhood thing from home to ward off evil. "There are no wolves in Iceland, Ran," he said.

Grim, who was on my back, woke and began to cry.

TWENTY-SIX

GULLI WAS THE FIRST to see them. He'd been sitting astride the roof, consolidating my repairs. He dropped his hammer and slid down in a shower of nails.

"They're coming, Agnar Thorfast! They're coming!" Gulli's voice was not long broken and it rose quickly to a screech.

"Are they now?" Agnar asked, putting his large hands down on Gulli's shoulders. "Then it's time to fight them."

Gulli nodded.

"You come with me to Mord. He'll have a spear for you, and maybe a knife."

I glanced at Gulli and found his face alight with pleasure and excitement. Gulli, who was no match for anyone. Did he not know, I wondered, that the best the fight could bring a lad like him was a quick death?

Agnar and Mord handed out weapons. Every man got at least a spear, and some had swords as well. The free men had shields and helmets. I had my own spear, which had been Amma's, and I had kept it sharp.

"Don't cry, Ran," Gulli told me, running past. "We'll beat them easily." I had not known that I was crying till he said that.

Sigrid and I rounded up all the children and put them in the grain store, under the floor, with Asa's old mother and two slaves who were pregnant. I noticed that Sigrid put Slodi in the middle of the children. I did the same with Gudrun and Grim. "Keep them safe, Allfather," I begged. "Don't punish them because their mother ran away from you."

None of the children cried. The women were already feeding them sips of a sleeping draught Asa kept. If the fighting went the wrong way, their best chance of escape lay in silence. There was no time to hold them, kiss them, touch their soft skin, smooth their hair. There was not time for anything. I ran back up the wooden steps into the hall. I could not see for tears, and shouted above the noise of shouts to Toki. He came to me through the crowd.

"They're not to be left down there, if we lose," he said. "Promise me, Ran. Not in the dark. If we look like losing, take them and run. Go with Sigrid. Don't leave them in the grain store to be taken. Ulf has made Sigrid promise too."

I promised. I took Thor's silver hammer from around my neck and dropped the worn thong over Toki's thick red hair. He gave me his knife, which he had sharpened for me. We held each other close, close, for a moment. Then he took his harp and walked out among the fighting men.

"Protect him, Thor," I prayed. "He's in your hands." I

prayed to Odin, too. "Protect him, Odin Allfather. It wasn't his fault that I didn't come to you at Sessing; it was mine. I wasn't ready. I am now."

I went to stand by Asa with the other women. We could hear the wolf howling, and men's voices, and feet running on the snow. Then shouting and the ring of metal. And Toki's music, clear and true, climbing above the sound of shouting and swords.

All the men were outside now, packed in behind the wall. We women moved forward to block the doorway. Half a dozen of the raiders were on top of the wall, and more were over it, inside the yard. Sigrid's Ulf was the first man to fall. He always was a slow man. He went down grunting with a spear through his chest almost at once. A thick gout of dark blood splashed across his sheepskin, the other man wrenched at his spear to free it, then bent to cut Ulf's throat. I glanced across to Sigrid and saw that she was screaming, though I could not hear her above the noise of battle. She had no weapon so I passed her Toki's knife.

Gulli, who had been tucked in behind Ulf, caught an axe blow in the shoulder and lay where he had fallen. Blood ran down his sleeve, pooled in the snow, and froze. If nobody finished him, he would take some time to die. His small face was clenched and yellow, like beeswax. His eyes were open but he made no sound.

Toki climbed up to stand on a great blade of rock that pushed through the bloodied snow close by the wall. A small wind took his red hair off his forehead. His dark eyes looked away into the distance. From his hands the music rose golden and warm and wild. I was watching him so closely that I saw him clear his throat and swallow. Then he put down his harp and sang. He sang about Valhalla, the Hall of the Slain, whose walls are made of golden spears, whose roof is of golden shields. There are five hundred doors, and each is wide enough to let a thousand men through, walking side by side. From that great hall the Valkyries ride out to find fresh heroes on the battlefields of Midgard. And each man as he dies, if they have chosen him, sees them and knows that he is chosen.

Toki sang with his head back and his black eyes looking away at nothing while arrows flew and blades bit all around him. Any one of the raiders could have scrambled up and killed him with axe or sword. They could have shot him full of arrows. But they did not. They must have thought his courage an enchantment. He made them frightened, and us brave.

The raiders were in over the wall and slipping on the red snow in the yard by the time I looked up and saw Vigut watching me. I saw the wolf also. He had the wretched beast dragged up against his legs on a rope, half throttled, a leather strap tight around its muzzle. Its ears were flat against its skull and its tail curled down around its flank. It wanted to crouch down with its thin ribs to the snow. Each time it tried, Vigut jerked it back onto its feet.

Beside him stood a child, dressed it rich furs, its face ancient and menacing.

Vigut looked from Toki to me. He stared a moment, then winked at me and glanced back at Toki, high on the rock, hair streaming in the wind, voice soaring. He smiled, handed the wolf's rope to the child, and drew his sword.

Asa screamed close beside me. I looked away from Vigut for a second and saw Mord lying in the snow, still moving, while a man chopped at him. I thought of my son, Grim, below in the grain store. Rage choked me and I hoped he'd die before he grew into a man to die like Asa's son down in the snow with an axe cutting his life away.

Agnar had seen Mord die and ran to kill the man who'd killed his son. Flight and Fiddle were close behind him, Flight wounded but still on his feet, Fiddle unscathed, stabbing with his long spear and slicing with his knife. More of our men than theirs were lying in the snow. Something made me look up into the sky and I saw that Thor was sending us another storm. Too late, I thought. This one will only serve to bury us. I looked back at Toki. Vigut had fought his way to the bottom of Toki's rock.

Something cold hit my foot. I looked down and saw blood running, and an arrow. I stumbled and fell into the snow. Sigrid pulled at my arm.

"They'll be coming in on us any time now," she said. "We must take the children and run."

"I cannot run, Sigrid," I said.

"I know."

"Take them with you, Sigrid."

"I will."

"Protect them."

"Like my own."

She tore a strip from my dress, pulled out the arrow, and tied up my wound, all in a few seconds. Then she kissed me on both checks and ran back inside the hall.

I looked back to the rock. Vigut was up there, breathing

into Toki's face. Toki was still singing. I could see that he expected his death to come at any time. I screamed and Vigut looked toward me, smiled, and pushed his blade to Toki's throat. I saw his dark eyes close, and his harp spin away down the rock. Vigut dropped a noose of leather over his head and tugged it tight around his chest, trapping his arms. He jumped down off the rock, jerking Toki behind him.

Neither of them noticed Kon, ears and tail flying, lips drawn back from old, blunt teeth in fury. He took off, red mouth open, all four feet off the ground, and hurled himself at Vigut's chest. His own weight carried him straight onto Vigut's sword. He died happy, as a good dog should, sure that he was about to sink his teeth into Vigut's throat.

Vigut pushed his limp body off his sword with the toe of one boot and brought the handle of his axe down hard on Toki's forehead. Toki crumpled into the snow, a thread of scarlet snaking over his face and down into his beard. Vigut kicked him to make sure he would not rise, then turned and looked for Agnar.

TWENTY-SEVEN

THE STORIES WE HAD heard about the raiders killing everyone were wrong. They had an eye to profit. They killed who they must, to show who'd won, and drove the rest into the hall.

Agnar was wounded, but still alive. Vigut tied him and Asa back to back and fastened them to the roof post by the fire. Flight and Fiddle huddled close by, also tied, among those dozen or so slaves and laborers, men and women, who remained alive. Toki lay propped against a bench and Vigut let me see to him. No doubt he was keen to have his own prize singer, like all great men. The blood had dried on Toki's forehead and his skin shone blue behind it where Vigut had hit him.

I leaned down and put my ear against his lips. "Why are you here?" he croaked. "You promised me."

I bent, as if cleaning his face. "I'm wounded. Not much. In the foot. Sigrid took them."

He turned his face away and I left him. There were others

dying for want of a bandage. A slave is worth more than a corpse, and none of Vigut's lot tried to stop me. They were a poor lot, dirty, thin, and wretched for the most part, with one or two obvious bullies among them. You could see they were glad that the fighting was over. If there was any fun to be had with the prisoners, it would not be yet.

The next time I looked up, the child in furs had come into the hall and was standing on the table. The wolf, on a long leather thong this time, crouched underneath the boards, trying to chew something through its muzzle. The child took off his heavy cloak and dropped it on the floor. He took off his catskin hood and I saw that he was not a child. Vigut had brought Brokk with him.

Brokk walked up and down the table for a minute, sniffing. He pulled his snakeskin rattle out from underneath his shirt and shook it quietly. He told one of his men to build the fire up, and I noticed then that it was nighttime and dark. Sparks jumped from the fire pit as wood was thrown on. Agnar was closest to the fire. He turned his head aside from the heat. Brokk smiled but said nothing.

He hopped down off the table and yanked at the thong. The wolf crept out and stood beside him, cringing. Brokk shortened its lead and undid its muzzle. He began to walk the creature up and down, lengthways and sideways, quartering the hall. I crept across to Toki, quietly, and squatted on the floor beside him.

The wolf stopped over the grain store. It lowered its muzzle, sniffed, and scraped at the wooden planks of the floor. The hall grew silent. I could hear the creature's long claws clicking on the wooden boards. Somewhere a woman's courage failed her, and the sound of weeping came out of the darkness.

Brokk jerked on the wolf's lead and nodded. Two men came forward, one with a sword, the other with an axe. They pulled the two slaves out first, one screaming, the other silent. They glanced at Vigut and pushed the women over to the other prisoners. Next came Asa's mother, blinking in the light, her back bent double from the long hours crouched under the floor. Vigut drew a line under his throat with one finger. There was a roar from Agnar and a cry from Asa. I shut my eyes, and when I opened them again the old woman was on the floor, her throat cut, her life almost gone, a quiet rattle coming from her chest. Asa was shouting something. Agnar was trying to comfort her but he could not get his arms free.

One of Vigut's men lowered himself into the grain store and began passing up the sleepy children. Women began to scream, and men to shout.

"Damn you," Toki begged. "Tell me what's happening!"

"They've found the grain store."

Two bewildered infants, bundled up into the light, blinked and set off toward their mothers. Vigut shook his head, and the man with the sword caught them and killed them quickly. Three older children stood staring, silenced, still with horror. Sif, who was the oldest of them, saw her parents, straightened her back, and stalked across to join them. Vigut let her go. She was old enough to keep. Two babies, wrapped like bales of cloth, lay on the boards where

Vigut's man had left them. I shut my eyes. When I looked back, the men were wiping their swords. Vigut told them to shut the women up. Brokk walked over, let himself down into the grain store, said something that I couldn't hear, and came back up.

"Not ours," I whispered into Toki's ear. "They have not got ours."

Toki moved his hand as far as he was able and held mine. We wept. I don't know about Toki, but I was not weeping for the children who had died in front of me, but for my own, my own.

"Queen of the gods," I prayed, "protect my children. Goddess of death, take who you must, but not my children."

One or two men called in hoarse voices from outside the hall. I thought I recognized Gulli's small voice, crying out for water, but I dared not move.

Vigut got up from Agnar Thorfast's chair. He had not changed at all. Same dark hair, glossy and thick. Same white teeth, broken at the front. Same eyes, greedy and fierce. Even his big blue cloak was the same.

"Food," he said. "Cut some of them loose."

Two of his men moved to obey.

"If anybody who's supposed to be cooking my foods runs away," Vigut told us, "they will be caught and brought back and strung up from a roof beam. And I promise you it will take them until tomorrow night to die."

He sat down and began to drink a horn of ale someone had brought him, raising it first to Agnar. He emptied it and held it out again, drank, and called me over.

"Well, Eaglebeak," he said. "You're still alive. I see you're keeping company with the blind musician. I heard he was in Iceland. Word of his music traveled north to Stad on Skagafiord. I guessed you had run off with him that night at Sessing."

Brokk wandered over, tugging the wolf behind him, hitched himself up onto the table, and sat watching me from small, cold eyes.

"Brokk guessed it too," Vigut went on. "It should have been your mother here with me, not you, Eaglebeak. Was it the wolf bite killed her? Brokk here thought it was you. He thought that was why Odin wanted you. Gullveig said it was her several times before she died, but fire will make people say anything. Brokk will know how to find the truth. It's his job, Eaglebeak."

I said nothing. I was sick with fear.

"I am a rich man now," Vigut said, smiling. "I should have a praise singer of my own. I have a following. And a ship too. I shall trade and grow richer." He raised his horn to Agnar Thorfast. "Your ship," he added. "And your harbor, and your hall. Your wife also, if I want her. But your daughter's prettier."

I began to understand, hearing him talk, that he thought we must all admire him now that he was rich. I think he even thought that Agnar Thorfast would admire him for being what he was—a man who knew how to fight, and how to make other men fight for him. He was looking at me now, waiting for me to praise him. He would have preferred my mother's praise but she was not here to give it.

I stared at him, unable to say anything. Agnar had begun

to bellow, telling Vigut that he had friends who would avenge all wrongs done to him, beginning with the death of Mord, his son. He reminded Vigut that rape of a virgin was a capital offense in Iceland. He said there would be many men pleased to carry out the sentence, court or no court, if Vigut touched his daughter Sif.

I knew it was important to please Vigut. If we angered him, more of us would die. Also, as long as he was happy he would stay here feasting. And the longer he stayed in Agnar's hall and feasted, the farther Sigrid could run. He was still looking at me and I knew that I must speak.

"Shall I prepare your food?" I said. "I'm a good cook."

"Are you, Eaglebeak?" He laughed. "Yes. See about my food. Brokk can do his business with you later. And some-one put those screeching women in the barn where I can't hear them."

TWENTY-EIGHT

THIS WAS DONE, but I could still hear Gulli's voice from time to time, calling for water. I looked up from the fire where I was making Vigut's supper. He looked well contented so I asked him if I could go out and bring the wounded in.

"There's none out there worth saving," he replied. "None that would fetch anything at market. I've looked. But if the noise troubles you, I'll send a man to quiet them."

One of his men stood up, took a long knife from his belt, and went outside. He came back in soon after, stamping snow off his boots, and I didn't hear Gulli anymore.

I asked for Flight and Fiddle to be cut loose, which they were, and sent them to the barn to fetch meat. I chose the best cuts and put them to roast over the fire for Vigut. The rest I boiled up in a big pot for his men.

"Queen of all the gods," I begged, "let Grim and Gudrun have found somewhere warm. Let them be safe and hidden. Queen of the gods, keep them safe. Hide them and let them live." The words beat in my head like a pulse until I grew afraid that Brokk must sense my longing and send his starveling wolf out across the snow, sniffing after my sweet Gudrun, nosing after Grim.

Presently Vigut called across to Toki, who still lay propped against a bench. "A song, music man! Get up and sing for me!"

Toki got up, fell down, and got up again more carefully. "Is my harp here?" he asked. Someone went out to look for it, taking a branch from the fire to light the way, and came back presently with the harp dangling from one hand. I could see from the white on his head and shoulders that it was snowing.

"Queen of the gods," I prayed, "let them find shelter from the storm."

Toki walked out to the middle of the hall, struck a chord, found two of his strings were broken, and told Vigut he'd need time to mend them. Vigut looked angry, told him to get on with it, and turned to Brokk.

"Where do you want the offerings made?" he asked. "Here from the roof beams, or outside?"

Brokk tilted his head back to stare up at the roof beams. "I think they'll hold," he said. "Allfather will not mind if we make our offerings indoors tonight, provided that we offer all he wants."

"And what might that be?" Vigut asked.

Brokk considered, head on one side, for a moment. He looked across at me.

"Allfather must have the hook-nosed bitch who jumped

down off his tree at Sessing. He must have the blind man too, because I think he helped her down. And he must take what brats they may have spawned. That much is owed to Allfather already, before we thank him for our victory."

"A pity," Vigut answered. "I would have liked to keep the music maker."

"In thanks for this hall we should offer also those who died in the taking of it. To ensure our holding it, Agnar Thorfast and his woman must hang from their own roof beams."

"And their daughter?" Agnar asked.

"I think there is no need to offer her as well," Brokk answered, with a smile.

Vigut's meat was ready. I went over to the chest behind the long table and fetched a plate, Asa's finest silver stamped with a pattern of twining dragons. I laid Vigut's strips of roasted calf meat on the plate and put it down in front of him. Fiddle filled his ale horn, and I went back to stir the stew. When it was ready I set it out in bowls all down the table for the men.

Our people were desperate for food but we were given none, nor any water. I stood behind Vigut's chair while he ate, ready to serve him. When he had eaten I asked him if he'd passed by Smolsund on his way from Sessing. He was busy picking bits of meat from between his teeth and did not answer straightaway. When he had finished he looked up and nodded.

"A few men got away from Sessing while we were burning it," he said. "That place was much too fine for a fool like

Finnulf. He had much wealth hidden there. I found it all before I burned the place."

"Was it you who took Sessing?" I asked, surprised.

"Of course. I was on my way to take it when I stopped at Smolsund. For old time's sake, because I knew your mother long ago. I lost her then because I was a poor man. I meant to keep her this time. I have the men and money now. But not her. Why is that, Ran?"

He was drunk, and near to tears. I did not answer.

"Two of those who got out when we were burning Sessing ran to Smolsund. I found them there when I went back to get my horse. They told the old crone, your grandmother, that I was party to the burning. They didn't think I'd be so close behind them. I killed them both, for telling, and that old fool of a servant. Your old grandma caught a spear in her side and went out like a lamp in the scuffle."

I thought of Od.

I thought of Amma, of her small, light body and her crumpled face, then tore my mind away from pictures of her death.

Brokk cleared his throat impatiently and Vigut bowed to him, half mocking, half in earnest. He told someone to put out all the torches and the hall grew dark. Red light from the fire lit up the roof beams overhead. Somebody threw a rope up. "We'll give the gods the best first," Brokk said.

Asa died quickly, but Agnar's was a hard death. I held Sif tight in my arms till it was over.

Then Brokk came to me. He winked at me and waited, hoping, I think, for me to show my fear. "Well, gallows-thief," he said at last. "How many brats have you bred with the musician? And where are they? I know that they were not among those we have killed. I saw your face while we were killing them."

I looked away, saying nothing. He strutted over the dark floor of the hall to where Toki sat, patiently trying to mend his harp strings—which was a job I'd always done for him since we'd been together.

"How many bastards, music man?" he asked. "And where have you hidden them? One of you will tell me. Allfather will not be cheated twice."

Toki put down his harp but did not reply. Brokk sighed. "Listen, blind man," he said. "My name is Brokk. I can see in the light and I can see in the dark. I could see your children if I chose to look. But you will tell me where they are. And Fenris, my wolf, will tell me if you don't."

"Then let him tell you," Toki said, "for I won't."

"We'll see," Brokk said, quiet and calm. "We'll see."

Vigut's men began to look interested. Two of them tied Toki's arms behind his back, and Brokk pushed a knife into the fire to heat.

I let go of Sif and felt myself falling, but she caught me and held me in her arms just as I'd held her. There was nothing of the child left in her. I hid my face against her small, flat chest, and tried my hardest to hear nothing.

Wind gusted around the eaves of Agnar Thorfast's hall. It blew in at the door and set his body swinging. A little blood dropped down from his body and hissed into the fire. Brokk walked around and around, looking now and then from Toki to the fire, where his knife began to glow.

Fenris, poor starved creature, began to moan and whimper. Even the wolf feels pity, I thought.

But it wasn't pity Fenris felt. It was fear. Suddenly all the dogs were barking and yammering, and I felt the floorboards shiver under me. The whole hall shook, just once, as if it were a fly on the hide of an impatient horse twitching it off lazily in some summer meadow. Something peculiar happened to the air. There did not seem to be enough of it. Then came a noise, enormous, like thunder. I felt it strike my body like the big waves did in summer on the beach at Smolsund, when I was a little girl. It lifted me off my feet and threw me down onto the rippling floor. One of the roof beams cracked and burning thatch began to rain in on us.

I lay still for a second, feeling something scorch my shoulder. All around the hall people lay, crouched, crumpled, sprawled. There was a noise like water rushing, which came from underneath our feet and from the air above us all at the same time. The dogs were running out into the night. Vigut pulled himself back onto his feet and ran out after them. I leaped up and flew across the hall, pulled Toki up onto his feet, and dragged him out toward the barns behind the hall.

There came a roaring like the end of the world, and something cold squeezed all the breath out of our lungs. The roof of the hall lifted like the wing of a great bird. Fire whirled up through the rafters and rose into the sky.

A wall of water came down on us from out of the darkness, shining and solid like polished rock. There was no time to run. It tore Toki away from me. It threw me clear of barn and hall and everything, sucking me down, spinning me like a fish caught in the turning of the tide. I came up gasping, lungs bursting, and the sky was burning. Great clots of fire roared out of the top of Helga Fell, black rocks flew up like pebbles from a child's hand, veils of flame swept down the mountainside. Down I went again. Cold cut me to the quick, the current threw me up, and I cried out for Gudrun and for Grim. I felt myself slipping down and away and howled out Toki's name.

When I hauled my head out of the water all the fire was gone. The sky was full of dark smoke, and the stench of burning, hot ash hissed into the water around me, and my feet felt mud beneath them. The wall of water was gone, though a stream remained, dirty and ash-choked. I was lying half in and half out of it, I did not at first know where. Something had happened to my right arm and the wound in my foot had opened. I felt colder than I had thought living flesh could feel. I sat up, leaving my arm hanging where it seemed to want to stay, and looked around. The night was dark and growing darker. I could see no farther than my left hand. I was afraid to shout in case I might bring Vigut and his men down on me.

May I never suffer another such night. I crawled, dragging my torn arm with me, through black mud and black smoke, choking with some fiery stench, soaked and frozen, hopeless and heartless, looking for Toki. And did not find him till the morning.

TWENTY-NINE

TOKI WAS LYING WRAPPED around the base of a rock. His red hair was stained black in the mud. I tried slowly to peel it back from his face, to free his nose and mouth from vile, stinking mud. I tried to lay his limbs straight, but they were heavy, heavy, and he was so cold. Presently, I gave up trying to move him, and lay down beside him with his wet hair in my wet face, my good arm under me, and the other awkward against his chest, his broad, strong chest, the crisscross vessel of his ribs that held his heart. I felt nothing except my need to stay there with him. Grief came later and stayed for many a day.

Well. That was long ago.

But I still feel what I feel. I still remember how we learned each other's bodies in his bed before we went to Vegasund. I remember how he promised me a child each year in Iceland. I remember how he used to read my face with his hands. I remember his singing and the golden music of his harp the first time that I heard him play in the great hall at Sessing. I remember that he was gentle with his dog and his horse. Oh, I remember much, so much, and good it is.

But I've forgotten much also, more than ever I wanted to. Time does that. Time washes off the skin of life but not the pain and not the joy. They stay.

I got up at last and left Toki where he lay. The flood water had carried him a mile or more from Thorsdale, down onto the beach where the gray waves danced in from the sea. A cold wind blew the spray off their crests and sent it streaming back as they rushed forward, back out to the sea and Norway.

An old gray seal watched us from far out beyond the rocks. I prayed the tide would take his body soon, carry it out, and tumble it down through the cold, live seawater to Ran, my namesake. I turned his face toward the sea and left him. Then I began to look for Grim and Gudrun. I knew they could not have lived through that wall of water, but I searched.

At first I met no one. Thorsdale was destroyed and all the people with it, good and bad alike. I found the wolf with his lead wound around a fallen tree, drowned. Nearby was a bundle of drab rags that might have been his master, Brokk. I didn't look.

Ash covered all the land, and a dead gray rime. It looked like stone that had melted and set hard again. The mountain had burst open, spewing fire and rock onto the icefield below, melting that road of ice and letting loose a deadly torrent of ice water filled with bouncing, grinding boulders.

I must have eaten something, but I can't remember what. After two days I fell in with some stragglers from the north. They had been following the raiders south, I think, picking up what crumbs they left behind. They were cold and hungry and bewildered. One of them shared a piece of salt fish with me, a generous gift. She showed me where she was sleeping, in a half cave, between rocks, up on the hill to the west of Thorsdale. I remembered, when she showed it to me, that Sigrid sometimes used to come this way, perhaps to this very cave, to meet her lovers. We made a little fire there of willow twigs, and cooked fish we had picked up where they lay stranded when the flood went down.

Her name was Inga. She had lost all her family in a raid and was half crazy. She did not want to live but could not die, being tied fast to life by the thread that ties parents to their children. She ached to care for them, although she'd seen them die. I told her I was searching for mine and it seemed to comfort her to help me look. We walked all day, searching and calling, asking anyone we met for news of them. At night we crept back to our cave to sleep and woke each other with our nightmares.

On the third evening I found Gudrun's dress, a rag hanging in a willow bush, and I knew that it was time to end it. These things must be done properly. I would go down to the sea in the morning and swim. I would swim toward Norway, with the gray seals for company, until Ran in her mercy should carry me down.

The air softened that night, the wind veered around toward the south, and a fine spring rain beat into our cave. We set our little fire as far back as we could, and Inga made a soup of wild grasses and herbs. I sat bent over, picking lice out of my clothes, thinking nothing. Inga sat rocking and swaying on the other side of the fire. Both of us stank so we tried not to sit too close.

I leaned back wearily, trying to find a way to sleep. The wound in my foot throbbed, and my arm still hurt each time I moved, but at last I found a smooth, round knobble of rock to lean against. As I wriggled to get comfortable, something dug into my shoulder. A twig or a small stone. I reached back to brush it away, brought my hand around to the firelight to see what it was, and found that I was holding a flat stick. I might have flipped it on the fire to burn, but something made me look again, and I saw them. Runes:

ı ı ↑ ↑ ↑

I did not speak. I did not take my eyes off that chip of wood nor the lines cut in its surface. I did not ask myself how long it had been there, nor where the children might be now. I did not ask whether they still lived. Sigrid, Slodi, I read. Gudrun, Grim. Alive. I turned the chip over. On the other side was one more character, repeated twice:

↑ ↑

Frey's Field. I shook Inga awake and showed her what I'd found. She could not read the runes, but I read them for her and told her what I thought they meant.

"We must go now," I said. "At once. Get up."

"It's dark," Inga said gently. "You must wait till morning. If you go now you may fall down a hole and never get there."

"I want to go!" I shouted, shaking her. "I want to go now! Let me go!"

She took my hand. "You shall," she said. "I will come with you, as soon as it's light."

She was right, of course. Incredibly, I slept before the light came. I dreamed of Gudrun running, running with a wolf behind her, and woke screaming.

It took us two days to reach Frey's Field because we were so weak by then. It seemed impossible to me, but nothing much was harmed up there. The horror of Helga Fell had struck only a few valleys, leaving Frey's Field standing where it had always stood, with the hill at its back and the valley at its feet. Why did we leave? I thought. Why did we leave?

I could not run, I could not even walk, but stood staring up at the stone hut, seeing smoke curl up from its chimney, my need for Toki almost choking me. Surely, if I waited, he would walk out through that door with Kon at his heels. It was long and long before I could believe he never would again.

Instead, Gudrun, my sweet Gudrun, came trotting out with Sigrid behind her. I tried to call but no sound came. I could not raise my hand. But my longing and my joy flew to her through the clear air. She looked up, smiled at me, and came tumbling down the path. My legs gave under me and I sat down on the wet grass to receive her. I held her to me with my good arm, and at first she smiled and laughed, but soon the storm of my grief and the power of my joy frightened her, and she began to cry.

Sigrid came up then, carrying a small bundle, took Gudrun back into the comfort of her own strong arms, and gave me Grim to weep over instead. It did not take me long to make him cry as well, his small face reddening, his mouth drawing down into a line ready to bawl. I laughed, and shook my head, and passed him up to Sigrid also, and asked then, only then, for Slodi.

"Alive," she said. "Alive." She asked for Toki. I told her he was dead.

THIRTY

T HAT NIGHT, SITTING beside the fire in the
house at Frey's Field while we talked, Toki felt present
to me in all of his familiar things. Impossible to believe that
he would never now take down the ragged cloak that hung
in the corner and wrap it 'round his shoulders. Never now
lay bare with his knife a shape that only he could find, hidden in wood or bone he'd saved for winter carving. Never
call Kon, nor know that Kon died trying to defend him.

Sigrid cooked. Gudrun sat in my lap, her hand twined
into my hair, shivering with fear. I had to coax her to take
just a mouthful of food. I had no milk left in my breasts for
Grim, but he would not take the pellets of bread dipped in
goat's milk that Sigrid offered him. I let him suck, and he
brought my milk back in the end, so perhaps he was right
to refuse the goat's milk.

Inga stared into the fire. Her mind was far away, in the
north probably, where she lost her children and her man. I
doubt she even heard us talking.

"Tell me what happened, Sigrid," I began. "From when you took the children from the grain store."

"That was very bad, Ran. The old lady knew it meant we'd lost. Sif too. Some of the children understood as well. It was dark down there. I couldn't see their faces but I felt them pulling at me, Ran. I left them there."

We were quiet for a while. Grim sucked at my dry breast, arching his back now and then, pulling away from me, angry and unsatisfied. Gudrun sat as still as stone, her knuckles white from holding on to me. Slodi snored beside his mother, wrapped in an old cloak of mine. A tear from Sigrid's eye dripped from her chin and fell onto his forehead.

"I had to choose."

"It was brave already to take mine as well as yours, Sigrid. If you had tried to take them all, none of them would have gotten away. There was less time, much less than we'd expected, after you went and before they took the hall."

"It doesn't make it right with those I left."

"Of course not."

"I can't forget them, Ran."

"Do you want to?"

She shook her head. "No. But I must know what happened to them."

"He had them all killed, Sigrid. Even the old lady. He kept the slaves. Sif walked bravely out across the hall to stand beside her parents. Whom he also killed."

Sigrid wept, and spat on the fire in anger, and wept again at what was done to the children in the grain store.

"I knew him, Sigrid. He was the man who came to

Smolsund and courted my mother and went with us to Sessing. It was he who burned Sessing, and later Smolsund. He killed my grandmother."

"Is he dead now?"

"Surely."

"I hope so. I felt the ground shaking after I ran. I heard the noise and saw the fire in the sky."

"Where were you?"

"Running. Running, with Slodi clamped under one arm, and Grim under the other, and poor little Gudrun holding tight to my skirt, half dragged along, until I hauled her up onto my back and there she clung, crying and calling for you, Ran. I went pelting up the valley at the back of Thorsdale, and up the hillside to the cave you found the rune-stick in. I put Grim and Slodi down there in the back of the cave, both of them yelling. Gudrun and I crept to the front and looked out just in time to see a cliff of water, black and shining, go roaring down the valley. It cracked the great hall at Thorsdale like an egg."

"It killed Toki. But it spat me out. I don't know why."

"I cut the rune-stick as an offering, Ran. I was sure that you were dead."

We sat silent for a long while after that. Gudrun slept in my lap with her brother beside her. Slodi woke, cried, then slept again. Sigrid and I watched them, and looked at one another sometimes, in the low light from the dying fire. There was nothing more to say. Sleep came soon after.

Inga died that same night, while I lay sleeping between my children and Sigrid lay curled around Slodi. I woke when she rose from the sleeping platform. I thought she'd gone out to relieve herself. I must have slept again at once, not missing her.

Sigrid found her in the morning, hanging from the eaves behind the house. We cut her down and buried her and set a smooth gray rock over her body. I still offer there.

Life came back to me too fast. I was not ready for it. But there was work to do, as there is always work to do. Children to feed. Goats to milk. Hens' eggs to look for. Fish to catch. Sheep to fetch in from out on the hills. In spring there would be planting, and wild birds' eggs to gather. First there was winter to live through, snow and more snow, and every now and then a stranger at our door, half dead and needing food and shelter.

We asked everyone who came if they knew anything about Vigut and Brokk and the rest. Everyone said the same—they must have drowned when the glacier melted and the flood hit Thorsdale. I would have been happier if I could have seen their bodies and known for certain they were dead. Even without Vigut, we knew that we might have to fight to keep Frey's Field. The land was like that in those days. It is quieter now.

Gudrun asked over and over for her father. At least she could remember him when she was little. Now, I think, she has mixed memory with things that I have told her. Grim remembers nothing of that time; he was too young. There was not a night we didn't weep from tiredness and sorrow and anger. But we managed till the spring, and life grew easier then, although the work was harder.

I still think of Inga sometimes. I took Grim's first tooth to her, and Gudrun's baby dresses. Later, much later, I took a portion of Gudrun's wedding feast and, soon after that, wine from the christening of my first grandchild, Gudrun's daughter—for we are Christians now and have new gods, though we do not forget the old ones.

I set up a fine stone to Amma, and carved the runes myself. It faces out to sea, as Amma liked to do at Smolsund when I was a girl.

Toki's stone is above the beach at Thorsdale, where I found his body. It says:

RAN RAISED THIS STONE

IN MEMORY OF TOKI

BEST OF MEN.

HIS MUSIC WAS AS SWEET AS HONEY

AND HIS COURAGE NEVER FAILED.

EPILOGUE

THERE WAS A DRAGON in the sky last night. It flamed across the red west from the mountains to the sea. Its eye glowed like an ember in the darkness of its face, but I was not afraid.

Today I ride down to the harbor below Thorsdale to take ship for Norway. Grim has found two places in the ship he serves in. He works a trading vessel between here and the Sheep Islands. He has a wife, and a child coming. He'll leave the sea and settle at Frey's Field, once the child is born. He does not know that yet, but it is what his wife has told me, and I'm glad. He's been across to Smolsund. He's made good the damage Vigut did, and now the house stands empty.

Gudrun sailed to the new lands they call Green, though I hear that they are white with snow often enough. She went with her man and their children, five summers back. She's a singer, like her father. I miss her.

They have rebuilt the great hall at Thorsdale; Agnar's brother's son lives there. He is a good man, like his uncle.

Sigrid moved farther north, with Slodi, but he's away at sea for half of every year now. I have been north to visit and she's come south to Frey's Field more than once. I owe her more than ever could be paid. She knows I thank her in my heart each day for her courage and her kindness. I hoped she'd come, when I sent word to tell her I was leaving. She will bring Amma's garden back to life, and I'll keep goats and chickens.

We'll be home at last.